THE SASSY NANNY DILEMMA

ELIZABETH SAFLEUR

Elizabeth SaFleur LLC
PO Box 6395
Charlottesville, VA 22906
Elizabeth@ElizabethSaFleur.com
www.ElizabethSaFleur.com

Edited by Trenda Lundin, Chas Patrick
Cover design by Jan Meredith

ISBN: 978-1-949076-42-4

Thank you to all the readers who shared their great parenting advice and "hacks" with me as I was writing this story: P Workman, Steve Hedges, Celina Stone, Sue Philips, Maretha, Dani Bartolotta, Julie Touchstone, Donna Stapleton, Debi Rayne, Bénédicte, Nicki, Timothea Pratt, Janice Packard, Lillian Kazmierczak, Melani Bannister, Pam Raver, Patti Dinger. Sorry if I missed anyone!

Adelaide thanks you, too!

Keep in touch with Elizabeth!

News From Elizabeth, my email newsletter, is the best way to find out about my new releases an gain access to free bonus content and more.

Sign up by going to elizabethsafleur.com

You can unsubscribe at any time. I never add anyone without their permission, and I don't share my newsletter subscriber list with anyone ever. Well, maybe with my fur baby, but he can't read so…

Enjoy The Sassy Nanny Dilemma!

XO,
Elizabeth

1
———

Adelaide held up her lifeguard certification paper against the light and studied the dusty footprint across it. Ashton Scott had enormous feet—like, seriously, a size fifteen or maybe even a sixteen. They matched his booming voice cutting through Mrs. Dexter's closed office door—a door she was walking through when he'd elbowed his way inside.

Before she could say a word, he'd thrust a child her way, spouting, "Watch her," and, "Five minutes," and, "Thank you," before shutting her out of the office.

The little girl squeezed Addy's hand. "Sorry my daddy got your paperwork dirty."

She smiled down at her. "A little dirt never killed anyone."

"I'm not allowed to get dirty."

"Oh, no?"

"But sometimes, I do." She lowered her voice. "By mistake."

"That's what soap and water are for." Addy winked. "They need a job, too, ya' know."

Her dimples deepened as she smiled up at Addy, which only made the moppet more frickin' adorable.

She had dark hair and Ash's ice blue eyes—blue eyes that fired when he honed in on her Practically Perfect Nannies T-shirt and left his daughter with her.

So bossy. Still hot. And a father, of all things. He also clearly didn't recognize Addy—at all.

How was he back in little old Moorsville anyway? She'd missed all the good gossip during her three months in the North Carolina Outer Banks with a family that, quite frankly, did not appreciate her as they should have. Three kids under the age of seven plus beach sand? No wonder their mother put vodka in her orange juice every morning.

Addy was going to kill her sister Scarlett for holding out that Ashton Scott, the famous attorney to A-list celebrities, returned to his hometown—*their* hometown. The sister code demanded that kind of dish was shared immediately.

Another long string of words—"…inexcusable, indefensible, you will fix this…"—boomed in the man's deep baritone from behind the door.

Addy winced, and her certificate crinkled in her hand. He had a voice that could wake his ancestors. "He doesn't sound too happy in there. I guess he didn't like your last nanny?"

The little girl took Addy's hand again and swung her arm back and forth, taking Addy's with her. "I dunno."

Addy freed her hand, shoved the certificate back into her folder, and left it on the waiting room chair. She retrieved something far more important—the bag holding the best pie on the planet.

Lordy, let there be no damage from when she dropped it. Or rather, when cranky-but-gorgeous Ash muscled his way past her causing her to drop the bag. Mrs. Dexter loved her sweets, and Addy needed all the goodwill from her boss she could get today.

She dropped down to a crouch. "What's your name?"

The little girl held out her hand for a handshake. "Maribelle Louisa Scott."

Addy's hand engulfed hers. "So, Maribelle Louisa Scott, do you have a nickname?"

"That child."

Ouch. A deep, sharp pain arrowed straight through her heart. "We're going to have to come up with something better than that. How about…" She tapped her finger on her lips. "Princess Maribelle?"

Maribelle sucked in a breath and her little rosebud lips dropped to an 'O.' She snapped them shut and cocked her head. "Can I be a queen?"

This was her kind of child. "Nice to meet you, Queen Maribelle."

Addy rose and peered at the folders lined up on the receptionist's desk. Terrie was so sloppy, leaving them out. She was probably on one of her two-hour lunch breaks. So, Addy wouldn't feel bad about what she was about to do—take a quick peek at Maribelle Louisa Scott's intake form.

A quick scan revealed no food allergies, special diets, or health issues for her. Something called the Genius Kid's Diet was listed. "Excellent." The brain needed glucose. So, universal permission granted.

Addy looked down at Maribelle. "You like pie?" She should have brought more than two pieces, but she could beg for a second chance from Mrs. Dexter sugarless. Queen Maribelle needed a pick-me-up.

Maribelle peered over the edge of the bag. "Never had it." She lifted her incredibly dark eyelashes. "I usually get an apple for dessert."

"What? Never had pie?" *Who was this child? And why were they torturing her?* "Well, no time like the present. Yummy cherry or…" She lifted out the paper cone holding the blueberry. "Yummy blueberry?" Both were fruit, after all.

Maribelle assessed the cherry and wrinkled her nose. She pointed at the blueberry one.

Adelaide placed the paper cone that held the pie piece between Maribelle's little hands. "Let me guess, you're, what, sixteen? Seventeen? Almost ready for college?"

The little girl giggled. "I'm six years, four months, and three days old." She took a big swipe of the blueberry filling with her tongue. Her baby cheeks dimpled again. She opened her mouth wide and bit into the pie, instantly coating her chin and nose with dark purple filling. "Mmm. Shank you."

Crumbs blew out of her mouth, dusting the front of her white apron. Maribelle's wardrobe was another thing that did not compute about this whole scenario. She wore a little blue dress with ruffles on the hem and a white apron on top like Alice in Wonderland—like a *doll*.

"You are so welcome." Addy took a small bite of the cherry. Once the pie was out of the bag, it demanded worship.

"Do you want to be my new nanny?" Maribelle took another bite. "We just moved here. From New York."

"We'll see." She'd hoped to be *someone's* nanny—provided Practically Perfect Nannies didn't fire her.

It was not her fault Mr. Emerson got a face full of flour. It was the closest thing she could reach when he backed her up into the pantry.

Addy took another bite of the cherry. "So, New York. That's exciting."

"Yep. And Daddy's throwing a big party tonight." Maribelle's little curls bounced everywhere as she took another bite of pie. "Cook says he's a big fish."

A chortle flew from Addy's mouth. "Fish, huh? And let's not talk with our mouth full."

Addy studied the little girl. She knew one day Ashton Scott would do great things—far away from here. But when she saw his picture splashed on the cover of Forbes last year, she'd never guessed he would ever have a *child*. The headline, 'The Exalted One,' didn't exactly speak to runny noses and playdates. Guys like him went out with supermodels and sewed condoms onto their dicks to ensure pregnancies were off the gold-digger menu.

Addy pointed at her T-shirt and the black outline of a woman holding an umbrella. "You think he wants someone practically perfect?"

Maribelle gave off a cute little snort and swallowed. "Daddy says no one is perfect. But say you have an em-bee-yay. That's what everyone tells him."

An MBA, huh?

The door cracked open, and Addy shot to standing.

Ash stopped short in the doorway, filling it—like, his head nearly hit the top of the door opening. "I'll just have someone from New York fly down," he grumbled.

His nostrils flared at seeing her. His gaze alone must freeze his legal opponents' nuts right off.

He gazed quickly down at Maribelle and then back up at Addy. "Thank you for watching Maribelle."

"Daddy, Adelaide can be my new nanny." She bounced up and down. "I got pie!"

He straightened his suit and honed his gaze on Addy. Oh, yeah, the magazine cover did not do this man justice one bit. No wonder Maribelle was blessed in the genes department.

Addy dropped her pie into the bag, dusted her hands on her jeans, and jutted out her hand. "Hi. Adelaide Bloom. So, I understand you might need someone and right away?" He probably was someone who appreciated efficiency.

His head cocked at hearing her name. Maybe he did remember their one and only brief encounter?

He returned her handshake. "Ashton Scott. Maribelle, let's go."

Okay, he hadn't a clue who she was. "Maribelle tells me you're looking for a new nanny."

Mrs. Dexter darted out of her office. "Mr. Scott, no need to bring someone in from the New York office. Adelaide was who I was waiting for—as a stand-in for this evening. You wouldn't want to cancel your party over this little glitch."

"Little?"

Oh, yes, his eyes had nut-freezing abilities, alright. Like a male model staring at you from a high-end business suit ad. She prayed her panties wouldn't slide right down to her feet.

Mrs. Dexter's eyes widened at Addy. "Adelaide, you just got back in town?"

Addy knew exactly what her eye bulge transmitted: *You're not fired yet... so long as you play along.*

"Sure did." And, really, it was not her fault she was back. Mrs. Emerson was as insecure as a cat in a room full of rocking chairs and was convinced Adelaide *lured* her husband to their pantry. But it was Addy's word against hers —the story of her life.

She hooked her arm in Mrs. Dexter's. "All sorted out with the Emersons. Back to being available." Janet Emerson was probably filing for divorce right now, but good riddance. "Mr. Scott, I just met Maribelle. She's wonderful. We can have our own little party tonight. Isn't that right, Maribelle?"

She jumped up and down and a glob of blueberry landed on her shoe. "With pie."

Ash eyed Addy. "My daughter doesn't eat... pie." An honest-to-God sniff came out on the word "pie."

Maribelle took another huge bite. "It's weally goof."

His eyes sliced to Addy's hand, still holding the paper bag. She lifted it up to him. "Want some? The cherry will rock your world. Peppermint Sweet is the most amazing bakeshop. You probably know all about it since it's down the street—"

"No." He waved the bag away. "Good day, ladies."

Maribelle swallowed fast and gazed quickly up at Addy. "Em-bee-yay."

A crack in Ash's steel face formed. His lips formed a small smile which he beamed down at Maribelle, and his eyes shone with pride.

A tell-tale pang went off in Addy's heart. It was the twinge she always waited for when assessing a family dynamic. Did they love their kids? Were the kids happy? But did this family need her?

Clearly, he loved his little girl, and Maribelle knew it by the way she smiled up at him. She seemed happy. But her father's understanding of six-year-olds? Not *allowed* to get dirty? Ha!

Addy was perfect for them. Bringing normalcy to parents obsessed with being perfect themselves was her specialty.

Not only that, being able to nanny for *the* Ashton Scott? He was Grumpy McGrumpy, but working for him would look great on her resumé.

She had to act quickly. "I don't have an MBA, but I *do* have all the necessary certifications." She grabbed her folder that held her resumé and her updated lifeguard certification. At least something good came out of her three-month stay in the Outer Banks.

She handed him her folder. "I'm just back from working with a family Beach all summer. I can get sand out of places you don't want to know about. Baby powder. Does the trick every time. And I love kids."

He arched an eyebrow. "Well, that would be a prerequisite, don't you think?" He opened her folder.

"Yes, of course." This man was going to play hardball, wasn't he? "Mrs. Dexter, perhaps the Gerard family could get someone else? I realize it's last minute and all..."

Mrs. Dexter's brows furrowed. Okay, it was a little lie. No

Gerard family waited with open arms for Adelaide Bloom. Most families had secured their nannies long ago for the upcoming school term, but a Big Fish required a little reeling in—mostly with some good, old-fashioned FOMO.

She pointed to her certification paper on top. "That's my recently renewed lifeguard certification. I can pull a grown man out of a riptide…" she snapped her fingers, "…like that. I once even punched a fish."

He peered up at her. "And why would you do that?"

"It got too close to one of my kids when I was with a family in St. Martin." Addy smiled down at Maribelle. "And it was a very *big fish*." She glanced back at the big fish standing in front of her. "Huge. Like that." She pointed at his footprint on her certification.

"My apologies for…" He waved his hand over his foot stamp. "This."

"Yes, I understand getting dirty isn't acceptable."

Maribelle wiped her little hand on her apron, smearing it with blueberry drippings, as per the six-year-old code. Who puts a child in white anyway?

He sighed. "Your resumé says you're a relief nanny."

"Technically. It means I swoop in and relieve the main nanny. It's how I preferred it. But Mrs. Dexter and I were meeting about my next placement. It's time for a more permanent role. In fact, didn't you say there were two families in need?"

Also, technically true.

One of the families was her. Not her smartest move to give up her lease on her apartment when she was placed with the Emersons—her first real, full-time gig. Sleeping on her sister's couch was like sleeping on a patchouli-soaked sack of potatoes.

The second family was standing with her in the hallway—one very pissed-off Big Fish and a moppet in a tragic little outfit doing a damned fine job devouring pie as if she instinctively knew it'd be snatched from her any second.

"Mr. Scott." Mrs. Dexter stepped forward. "Adelaide is quite… popular."

Truth. But she'd rather be popular with her kids—not the delusional fathers.

He glanced at her resumé again. "CPR and first aid, basic survival skills. You have an associate degree in childhood psychology, and you've worked with…" He stilled and peered up at her. "Is this a typo?"

"Nope. Twenty-seven families."

He handed back her paperwork. "Relief nanny or not, job-hopping is a sign of instability and lack of commitment."

Ooo, grumpy and stern. "I'm experienced. Varied. Can now handle anything." What would impress Ashton Scott? Besides an MBA. "Like, I can make a costume out of leaves and twigs if needed. Science fair projects are no problem at all. Oh, and I can drive a tractor and an RV—and a horse."

Maribelle gasped. "You have a horse? Daddy, a horse!"

He heaved another sigh and pinched the bridge of his nose. "Mrs. Dexter, you'll have new candidates tomorrow?"

Mrs. Dexter swallowed and nodded.

"Then Miss Bloom may watch Maribelle tonight and tonight only. Maribelle starts at the Moorsville Girls Academy soon and I will need someone long-term. Someone seasoned, who has stayed with a family for at least five years. I'll not have my daughter get attached to anyone to have them fly off." He moved to turn away but stopped. "And no fish fighter required."

Addy dropped her arms to her side. "Well, you never know…"

He lifted his chin a little and peered down his perfect, Roman nose. Did his lips try to smile?

"You have one hour to get the paperwork assembled and,

Miss Bloom, I trust you have a car? Or a horse? If not, I can arrange for transportation."

"I can drive myself. Um, where?"

Mrs. Dexter turned pink. "The Scott Mansion, of course, dear."

A little hitch in her heart made her straighten. She hadn't realized the house was still in the family. After Mrs. Scott passed away she made a point of never needing to visit that part of town. "Oh, of course. I'm so glad you kept it and fixed it up, I mean—"

"Five o'clock. That enough time? Don't be late."

So much for small talk—and wanting her to answer him. "Yes, sir."

He leaned down and lifted Maribelle into his arms. "Okay, my little Belle, time to go home."

His head cleared the doorway by mere inches, and Maribelle waved her sticky little hand toward Adelaide. Man, he was going to be pissed when he saw the blue stains all over the back of his jacket.

She turned to Mrs. Dexter, who took a visible deep breath. How was the woman so calm? Ashton Scott was back in town, and he was back at his old family place. Addy wanted to bust out of her skin.

"Adelaide."

She swung her gaze back to Mrs. Dexter. Addy had to watch his exit—or rather, his wide back in that fantastically cut suit. Men didn't wear clothes like that anymore.

Mrs. Dexter frowned at her. Addy lifted the bag. "Pie?" Sugar was a mood lifter, and maybe she wouldn't notice the two bites out of it.

"No. Let's talk in my office."

Addy followed her inside. "How did Ash Scott end up here?"

"We do not gossip about our families. But since you're

being hired—on probation, of course—I can tell you. A week ago, I stopped hearing from Charlie, the nanny I had on standby. I don't know what happened to her. She is always so reliable." Mrs. Dexter looked down at her desk, fists pressed on the surface. "But she's not answering her phone, and you're all I've got on such short notice."

Well, Charlie's loss and Addy's gain. Scarlett was going to die when she heard who Addy saw today—in the flesh. And my, what flesh he had. A mountain of testosterone encased in a finely cut suit. Terrible nanny thoughts, but sue her.

Mrs. Dexter looked up at her. "I can't begin to tell you how important this gig is, Adelaide. And this is your last chance. I just got off the phone with Janet Emerson, and she refuses to give you a letter of recommendation. What happened?"

Addy crossed her arms. "Like I said on the phone, I never once gave her husband reason to look twice at me. I mean, have you seen the man?" She nearly shuddered at the memory of his hairy paunch hanging over his speedo. He was the dead opposite of Ashton Scott.

"Adelaide. You need to tone things down a bit. You are not there to gain attention. You should blend in with the family dynamic that is already established. You're officially on probation." She raised a hand, probably to stop the speech Addy had rehearsed all the way home from North Carolina. Mrs. Emerson had paid for a rental car so Addy was away from her husband's paunch—as far away as possible, as quickly as possible. Fine by her.

Mrs. Dexter lifted her chin. "I'm sorry, but it's the second complaint—"

"In five years. I know, it's two too many but…" Why was she explaining anything? No one believed a Bloom in Moorsville.

Mrs. Dexter's gaze ran up and down her. "Appearances

are everything to Mr. Ash. Get a clean shirt on and don't be late. You have one night to prove yourself."

What did they expect? Watch a six-year-old in a ball gown? She was wearing jeans and a Practically Perfect T-shirt to show she was official. Her shirt just had a little pie smeared on the front.

"I'll be the best nanny Mr. Scott has ever seen. He's going to want to keep me after tonight."

"We'll see. One night, Adelaide. That's it." Mrs. Dexter threw herself into her chair. "Men like him expect you to follow orders. Not exactly your strong suit."

She could follow rules. Well, some of them. The ones that made sense.

But his no pie rule? Someone had to make sure Queen Maribelle ate something other than apples for the rest of her life. No one should ever be without pie in their life—*ever*.

"Promise me you'll be professional."

Her? She was the epitome of professionalism. Most of the time anyway.

She turned on her heel. She had some Googling to do, some serious preparation—like finding out why Ash was back in town.

And as for being hired for only one night? She'd see about that because *game on*.

2

———

The drumbeat behind Ash's eyes would not quit. He squinched his eyes shut and rolled his shoulders before turning to his assistant. "Please, say you don't need anything from me."

"Nope. Got it all covered." Stevens turned to a group of men holding a stack of ridiculous pink boxes labeled with a Peppermint Sweet logo in a large oval sticker. "Put them in the kitchen. In the back."

Great. More pie. He faced his assistant. "That sugar shack is the caterer?" He'd had enough of that addictive substance foisted on him today.

"Oh, no, sir. That's dessert. Cupcakes." She gave him a wide smile. "I'll make sure all the evidence of them are gone by morning."

Finally—someone understood his rules. Thank God Stevens came to this ridiculous town with Ash. If he had to be back here—which he still doubted but was told he had few alternatives—he was going to make sure things stayed as normal as possible.

If that was even possible.

"Be sure to keep them out of sight until tonight, will you?" If Maribelle got one look at those boxes entering the house, she was bound to ask for more pie. His little Belle was no fool.

Damn Adelaide Bloom and her completely, wholly inappropriate pie handover to his daughter today. Her name was familiar, but he didn't have time to puzzle it out.

He stretched his neck. He needed to get to his office, return to some normalcy. "A babysitter is arriving any minute. Once she arrives, send her to my office."

"Yes, sir."

With any luck, he could avoid the girl altogether after the initial meeting. He didn't have time to sort through all her… *words*. She used sixteen when two sufficed. And he was too far behind in his schedule.

He'd only gotten a five-mile run in that morning. The Transom settlement was late and now coming in tomorrow, God willing. Then he had to suffer through this dreaded party tonight, some damned welcome thing his PR firm cooked up. In fact…

He turned in the doorway. "Where the hell is O'Connor?"

Stevens looked up from her clipboard. "Plane is delayed."

The man waited until the last second to swoop into place? Could he blame him? "Call him. He can chopper in if he needs to."

"From New York?"

What was up with all this questioning today? Maybe the southern air did something to people—even his most treasured assistant. "North Carolina doesn't exactly require an ocean crossing."

"Yes, sir. Oh, thank God. I thought they'd never get here." A white van pulled up in the circular drive, and Stevens jogged down the stairs to meet it.

Daisy's Delivers was splashed across the side of the

vehicle along with a woman's face painted underneath. The figure was in profile, lips pursed, an arc of daisies floating helter-skelter as if she was blowing them out of her mouth.

He should have imported the food and the flowers from New York. Hell, *he* should be in New York, not this godforsaken little town hosting a party.

He lifted his chin toward his assistant. "I'll leave you to it." He then headed to where he should have been all morning if it wasn't for the nanny screwup last night: his office.

His last caretaker for Maribelle had returned to New York after only two weeks in this sleepy little town. She'd left a note on his desk, on a napkin, of all things. Something about the nights being too still.

Could he blame her? He wouldn't have ever left Manhattan if it wasn't wholly necessary. He'd use it for what it was worth—a reset, a public relations recovery, and most of all, a breather for his little girl after losing her mother and being hounded like prey.

He turned to close his office door to shut out the dozen people traipsing through his house to set up for tonight's little shindig. Perhaps he should have set up his office upstairs and not in the old-fashioned parlor off the foyer. Fewer distractions.

A loud "Wow" cut through the air.

Adelaide stood in the front doorway, her eyes darting over the foyer. "The place cleaned up well."

She stepped inside and sent her face toward the ceiling. She moved in a circle as if inspecting the mural his mother had painted years ago—a pale pink, blue, and white sunset with little cupids peering over the fluffy clouds. Maribelle was enchanted with the scene so he'd left it despite his desire to take a paint sprayer to every inch of the place.

The woman righted her head and grinned toward him.

"Thanks for taking care of them." She pointed up at the ceiling. "I hoped someone would."

So, Adelaide had spent some time here. He shouldn't be surprised. His mother was always holding some garden party or holiday open house.

"Miss Bloom." He gestured for her to step inside his office. "You brought the contract?"

"Sure did." She lifted a cupcake bag. "Hungry? It's a low-sugar pumpkin pie. So, it's healthy, right?"

Time to set things right—immediately. "Pies are not food. Rule number one. No sugar."

She followed him inside. "Like none? Ever?"

"Sugar is poison." He rounded his desk and stood behind it.

She hooked her thumb behind her toward the dining room. "So, who are we killing tonight? I mean, all those Peppermint Sweet boxes…"

"Are none of your concern." He reached down and lifted the trash can toward her.

"Right. Okay." She rolled her lips between her teeth and released them with a pop. She walked over to the trash can and dropped the bag emblazoned with Peppermint Sweet into it. It made a loud *thunk*. "Done. Though, the pumpkin? Heaven on earth."

She returned to standing before his desk and handed over her folder.

He opened it, found the contract, and flicked the pages to the last one. "Signed. Very good. Now—"

"It has a clause in it—number 34—that says if you want me to stay on past tonight, I can. I mean, I will." She pointed at it. "Just initial clause 34."

"I see that." She'd read the contract. Interesting. But he should not find anything about her interesting. She was here to do a job.

"I'm sure Mrs. Dexter can find another placement for you after tonight. You seem quite ambitious."

"Oh, I am. In taking care of children. I won't let you down."

"Good. Now," he gestured to one of the club chairs facing his desk, "have a seat."

She took it and settled her bag. It was a huge monstrosity with a horse head on it—in sequins, of all things.

He stared down at Maribelle's schedule. Was it folly to think this woman would adhere to anything on it? Probably. But it was one night. "We are having a party tonight—"

"Yes, a welcome home party. Everyone is talking about it. By the way, I'm really sorry to hear about Maribelle's mother."

Of course. Wikipedia probably had an entry on it outlining all the sordid details. His head pounded anew with the headlines that'd plagued him for the last year. He couldn't erase them from his mind if he tried.

Supermodel Kate Trent dies in tragic Telluride car crash, paparazzi blamed

    World-famous supermodel's secret baby with A lister attorney
    Attorney to the stars wins child custody, loses everything else

As if the rags understood anything. "Yes, it was an unfortunate accident." Never mind he hadn't talked to Kate in years or even known about Maribelle until he got called to Kate's last will and testament reading a year ago.

He rose and began to pace. Adelaide continued to beam an annoying smile at him. "My daughter has been through a lot." He lifted Maribelle's schedule from his desk, sat on the corner, and handed it to her. "No mention of her mother or New York."

"Understood. How is she holding up?"

"As well as can be expected. You'll find she is exceedingly bright. Curious. And, unfortunately, the center of too much attention. That's why we're here."

As soon as the news about Maribelle's multi-million inheritance came out, every Tom, Dick, and Henrietta had oozed out of the woodwork wanting a piece of him, believing he had the keys to Maribelle's fortune. Kate had a bigger head for business than he could have imagined, and stellar protective instincts when it came to their little girl. He couldn't touch her money—ever. Hell, he didn't want it.

He pointed to the schedule she held. "Read that. Memorize it. It has her schedule, her allowable night-time activities… her diet." Maribelle living off catering food at modeling shoots? Despite Kate's good qualities, her lifestyle was not fit for raising a child. As if his was?

"No sugar, got it." Adelaide slowly nodded her head as she glanced at the paper. "She has quite the schedule." She'd pronounced it "shhh-edule," as if British.

"Order is important in this house. Maribelle must get used to it. She's enrolled in the Moorsville Girls Academy this fall—"

"Oh, that's a good school. I mean, your mother went there."

"Yes." My, the gossip mill was working overtime. Any discussion about his mother, however, would be nipped in the bud. "My daughter may be young, but she is very bright. She'll excel in their academic excellence program. The alumni network alone will give her options in the future."

The young woman nodded. "It's also diverse and focuses on self-esteem and empowerment."

Surprising she'd know that unless she herself was an alumnus. "You went there?"

A snorty twitter erupted from her. "Hardly." She then cocked her head at him. "You don't remember me, do you?"

"Have we met?" His brain sifted through old memories. Occasional summers at this old place, the usual holiday drive-bys, then back to the boarding school.

"Once." She waved her hand. "It's okay. It was nothing. I mean, I used to work here after school and weekends, mostly during the school year, and I know you weren't here often. But your mom frequently talked about her Moorsville Academy days."

A mental image of his mother floated by and was gone as quickly as it arrived. Kind of like their time together. He cleared his throat. "You knew my mother well?"

"She was kind to me."

His gut twisted with another faded memory but he had no time for it. "Let's discuss Maribelle."

Adelaide laid the paper on his desk. "She's adorable. In fact, I'd say Queen Maribelle is—"

"Queen?"

"It's her new nickname." One side of her mouth quirked up. "Much better than *that child,* don't you think?"

What was this woman talking about? "No one would ever call my daughter *that child.*"

"Someone did."

"Who?" He lifted his chin toward her. "Did you hear something? I won't abide by any scandal-mongering."

"I'm glad to hear it." She scoffed. "Gossip is poison. Worse than sugar. But perhaps her old nanny? Though, I don't think you'd hire someone who would ever do such a thing. I can tell." She squinched her eyes together as if studying him. "I'm a great judge of character. I know things about people right away." She snapped her fingers. "Like you're definitely an Ashton. It's distinguished."

Was she flirting? He turned, honed his gaze on her. Her face showed no signs of distress. Most of the time, the stare he'd perfected over the years was enough to make most people squirm in their seats. This woman just turned on another smile.

She was used to opening doors with her smile, wasn't she? Pretty girls often relied on their looks.

"About Maribelle. She is to be kept upstairs during the party. Strangers upset her." Though, she'd taken to this Adelaide Bloom right away. But again, she'd been bribed by pie.

"Whatever you want."

What he wanted was to get through this night. "This is critical. No surprise visits."

"Oookay."

"Something you want to say?"

"I got a *Flowers in the Attic* vibe there for a minute." A visible shudder shook her shoulders but then she raised her hands. "Not that I think you're anything like those people…"

She really thought he'd lock his daughter in an attic? "This house is large. She sometimes has nightmares. It's important you stick with her." He would not have her sitting alone upstairs in this unknown house with all the blustery voices downstairs. She'd been through enough.

Her face relaxed. "Oh, whew."

She honestly thought he'd lock his daughter away? She did. This woman's thoughts ran across her face like the electronic ticker tape display at the New York Stock Exchange. She was so unlike the women of New York who had perfected their masks by age twenty-five. The difference was damned disconcerting.

He stood, an urge to shake off some energy overtaking him. "You can stay until 11 pm?"

"Of course. And I can stay all night if needed."

"It's not. Any other questions?" *Please, say no.* He moved to the doorway. Stevens had to be close and could take over from here.

Adelaide glanced around his bookshelves. "You must be glad to be home. It's nice here."

"I wouldn't know." And he wasn't staying.

"I've lived here all my life. If you need anything or need to know anyone, I'm your girl."

"I won't be here long. Only to get Maribelle settled." If there was a God. He stuck his head out to the hallway and got an eyeful of an enormous wildflower display on the center table. "Stevens?" With any luck, his assistant was within earshot.

"This town has a way of seducing you to stay."

A proverbial red flag flapped at him like a matador trying to wave down a bull. *This* reaction from her he understood. But there would be no seduction in this town or otherwise.

He twisted to face her. "Miss Bloom—"

"Adelaide."

"It would be best if we kept to a formal arrangement."

She smiled widely. "Clause 34 is waiting for your signature."

"No, I mean between us."

She laughed.

He hadn't meant it as a joke, rather she'd get a clue. "Something funny?"

Her smile dropped. "No. It's just..." She rolled her lips between her teeth again. The twist of her mouth shouldn't have sent a hot jab through his body. The one that said he was a man and she was—dammit. She was Maribelle's nanny for one night. Nothing more.

"Yes?" He arched an eyebrow when she didn't finish her sentence.

She raised both hands. "You're not my type. Too high maintenance. No offense."

"No offense taken." If anything, her disinterest in him was welcomed. He again peered into the hallway. "Stevens?" *Where was that woman?*

"Because I gotta tell you," she sucked in a long breath, seemed to search for her words, "always having to look good with the nails and the hair and the outfits?"

What in the blazes was this woman talking about?

She rolled her eyes—a literal *eye roll*. "To be seen with you? I couldn't do it. Not even for you."

This woman would be a lot of trouble, wouldn't she? His headache continued to pound at him as if reminding him in Morse code he had little choice at the moment when it came to Maribelle's care for the night. They'd simply have to avoid one another. Problem solved.

Thank Christ Stevens finally appeared. "Show Miss Bloom to the nursery. Miss Bloom, meet Miss Stevens."

"Hi." She rose and smiled at Stevens. "Heads up. Pumpkin pie is in the trash. Still in the bag. Technically still good. Unless you're not allowed."

Stevens blinked back and forth between them, brows knitted together. "This way, Miss Bloom."

As Adelaide was heading out, he overheard her again. "I gotta ask. The no dirty rule? How strict is that? Because, a six-year-old?"

"She must remain presentable." Stevens' whisper echoed in the foyer.

At least someone in this house understood what was going to happen under this roof.

Maribelle was going to need a good sense of herself given the spotlight she'd inherited from her parents.

Unfortunately, this town was a safe place to hide her, let her heal a bit. It also would possibly help get his own reputation on track, according to the PR firm he'd spent a ridiculous amount of money on.

He had a lot of perceptions to reverse, starting with people believing he was a deadbeat dad who swooped in only for his daughter's fortune. A playboy who only cared about wine, women, and winning. Including his nanny, apparently, by the way she described her thoughts about him. Watch him prove them all wrong. Well, except for the winning part. That was in his blood.

He stepped over to the doorway, glanced up at the ceiling of cherubs and clouds, a fantasy depiction of Heaven and the afterlife. Such an optimistic scene. If only real life was that simple.

As Adelaide climbed the steps behind Stevens, her dark hair swung in time with her hips. A memory again tried to surface but didn't fully form. So, he and Adelaide had met before. Then again, he'd met a lot of people in his lifetime. But anyone connected with this house had been long buried —just the way he liked it.

3

___

Addy let her hand glide along the familiar mahogany banister as she followed Miss Stevens up to the second floor. How the woman climbed stairs in a pencil skirt, she'd never know. It was probably picked out by Ash because anything less formal was an affront to his standards.

Addy always knew Ash was going to live a big life far away from Moorsville. Well, he certainly had *grown up big*. He grew up into a ginormous, jaded, uptight, supermodel-chasing snob.

She should have been completely turned off by his holier-than-thou attitude—especially around sugar. Who throws out pie? But she wasn't. Rather, her lady parts jumped to attention like someone lining up on their first day of boot camp.

Dammit. Why did he still affect her? And really, could she have been any more awkward? Not her type? How about the other way around?

His very existence was wholly unfair. It only pointed out what other men were *not*.

He was gorgeous, talented if his client list she'd found

online this afternoon was any indication, and must have stock in some special pheromones by the way her hormones lit up listening to him get all tough and imperious with her in his office.

Maybe Addy's continued weakness for him was because she was back in the Scott mansion. She hadn't expected the house to be so soaked with memories from the past—something she'd worked very hard at avoiding, the most poignant one involving the very hallway Stevens was now leading her down.

It was the place she'd run into Ash all those years ago. The place of her greatest humiliation. A run-in he didn't recall at all. Once again, Addy was reminded she was merely the "sometimes maid's" daughter.

Except she was way more than that now, and Ash would soon learn it.

She had skills—ones he clearly needed. The man hadn't a clue about how kids worked, and Addy did. For one, dirt was good for you. It was the new Prozac, something he seemed in dire need of.

Maybe he wasn't perfect.

"You've known Mr. Scott long?" Addy might as well learn more about the grown-up Ash if she was going to be working for him.

"Yes."

"How do you like Moorsville?"

"It's fine."

"Maribelle seems super-smart."

"Yes."

Okay, dead end. "Do you mind if I—"

"Yes."

Miss Stevens didn't even know what she was going to ask on that last one. But how could she be surprised at the woman's reticence around chit-chat? Given the size of the tree limb stuck up Ashton Scott's butt, he'd likely forced Miss Stevens to sign an NDA that would have her give up her soul if she said anything other than "yes" or "no."

Miss Stevens pointed to a particular doorway. "You're not to go into Mr. Scott's room ever."

Okay, now all Addy could think about was opening the door. She mentally pictured a massive, king-size bed with big maroon velvet curtains like actual royalty. He probably laid on gray sheets that'd show off his naturally tanned skin. Had a drawer full of condoms—the good kind, not the cheap, rubbery, novelty, glow-in-the-dark kind one of her ex-boyfriends used. Ash would be classier.

Jesus. She'd already thrown herself back into the Ash Scott admiration zone. She shook her head slightly, as if that would shake loose some logic that might kick her lusty thoughts into submission.

Stevens gestured for her to step inside a room across from Ash's bedroom. She did but stopped short. She whistled into the space. The room was larger than her old apartment. Clearly, her memory about this house had some holes in it.

Stevens arched a perfect brow her way. "Something wrong?"

"I don't remember this room being so big, that's all. And so… Edwardian."

"What?" The assistant peered over her glasses at Addy like she'd spoken in some foreign language.

"The fireplace? And armoire?" She pointed at the huge piece of dark furniture. "Does anyone check for creepy clowns or ghosts at bedtime? Because if Maribelle can sleep with that, she's a better queen than me."

"I wouldn't know. Mr. Scott usually tucks her in," Stevens sniffed.

Addy glanced around to make sure Mrs. Scott's old antique china dolls with cracks on their faces were gone.

Also, the creepy paintings of children from the 18th century with eyes that followed you when you walked by. Those were etched into her memory for good.

Instead, tacked to the faded fleur-de-lis wallpaper were pictures of fairytale castles in a child's scrawl. Pirates stormed castles. Women in ballgowns held swords. That was some therapy being worked out right there, alright.

If this gig wasn't some kismet at work, Addy didn't know what was. Maybe that's why she was here.

Maybe she could finally lay to rest her brief past with Ashton Scott.

And more importantly, his child needed her. Her heart hadn't stopped panging all day as if beating out a special message. It was so odd. She always bonded with the kids she watched over, but Maribelle got inside her the quickest.

Before Addy could step further into the room, Stevens placed a hand on her arm. "Mr. Scott is very particular when it comes to his daughter."

You don't say.

"It is imperative you follow the books," she continued.

"Oh. Let me guess. *Perfect Parents, Perfect Child?*" Please, dear God, say no. She'd had enough of that ridiculous crapola shoved down parents' throats. Perfection was for Netflix, not real life.

Stevens' mouth screwed into a frown. "Of course not. *The Genius Child* series."

Addy did a reasonable job of tamping down an eye roll. Her mouth, however, couldn't help but give out a long *ooohhh*. She'd arrived in the nick of time, hadn't she?

Addy glanced around. "So, where is our little genius in the making?"

"I'm sure she's in here somewhere." Stevens waved her hand.

The room spanned nearly the length of the back of the

house. A six-year-old could get lost here. Which was probably why they found Maribelle in her closet, flanked by one huge, stuffed German shepherd dog and a giant, pink, fluffy rabbit.

"Thanks, Miss Stevens, I got this."

The woman wasted no time turning on her clickety-clackety heel and exiting.

"Hi, Maribelle. Whatcha doing?"

The little girl's knees were drawn up under her chin. She sported a fantastic mean girl face. It'd be as effective as Ash's nut-freezing stare if it didn't emanate from a child with supermodel genes. Shiny hair, blue eyes as clear as sapphires, and her skin? Totally wasted on the young.

A little huff left her lips. "Fortressing."

Addy stamped out the giggle attempting to rise in her throat. "Ooooh. Can I do it, too?"

"Okay, but you have to be really still or they'll find us."

"Who?" Addy sat down and scooted her bag next to her.

"All those strangers coming and going downstairs all day." She sank deeper into her pile of stuffed animals.

Addy glanced around the closet. Yep, as she suspected. All dresses—most of them with ruffles and prints with hearts and butterflies. "We're going to have our own party here. Just you and me. No one else allowed." She inched closer to Maribelle. "You have a nice room. Back out there." Addy gave a jerk of her head backward.

"I want yellow walls."

Addy let out a big gasp. "My favorite color."

Her face relaxed for a second, but it wasn't long before her brows furrowed again. "You're only saying that because I did."

"Pinky swear. Look." She opened up her black jacket and revealed her T-shirt that had a big yellow sun behind the

Practically Perfect logo. "Yellow is the best color. Hey, I have an idea."

She brought her bag to her lap and rummaged around. "I have lots of good stuff in here." She found what she needed, popped open the rolling stick of lavender oil, and rubbed some on her wrist.

She held out the stick to Maribelle. "Want some? It calms the soul."

Maribelle stuck out her arm. After rolling a big swipe on each of her wrists, Addy showed her how to rub them together. "Now, waft your wrists under your nose whenever you feel a little uneasy. It's magic protection oil."

Maribelle smelled each wrist.

"See? Feel better?"

"Maybe."

Addy rose. "Can I meet your dolls?" She'd passed a little table and chair in the center of the room. It'd been set up for tea with ruffled doilies like a Pinterest post. Thank the goddesses there were no creepy china head dolls sitting around the table.

Maribelle sank further into her pile of stuffed animals. "Not yet. I'm waiting until everyone is in the book room."

"The library? Is that where your dad hosts parties?"

She shrugged. "It's where the bottles are."

"Oooh." Addy sat back down. "Tell you what. I can help. Close your eyes."

After a long second, Maribelle complied. The delay was good. It showed she thought for herself.

"Now, imagine a magic cloak around you that protects you."

Her eyes snapped open. "Magic isn't real."

"Who said?"

"My daddy."

"Well, maybe he hasn't discovered it yet. You know, like Harry Potter."

Maribelle giggled. "Daddy is older."

"Well, you know how I have trouble with ages. So, close your eyes. I can get you a magic cloak that way."

She settled herself, cross-legged, and rested her arms on her knees like a little swami. "Will it be like the invisibility cloak from Harry Potter?"

"Maybe. This one is especially for you. Made for Queen Maribelle."

"It's yellow."

Very good, Queen Maribelle. Imagination. On. "Very pretty. Now, you have it on and pretend you are walking downstairs."

Her forehead wrinkled again.

"But remember, it's magic and no one can see it but you. And everyone is smiling and happy and they simply nod their chins at you. Like it's important to show respect."

She pouted. "And no putting their hands on my hair."

"That's right because the magic cloak won't let them."

Her eyes popped open. "What color is yours?"

"Mine is blue but with little daisies all over it." She hadn't thought about that in a million years. "But mine does other things."

"Like make you invisible? Can mine do that? So I can sneak one of the cupcakes." She huffed. "It looked like a lot. I wish we had some to go with our tea." She jumped up and grabbed Addy's hand. "I'll show you."

At the little table, Queen Maribelle was most definitely in her element. First, Adelaide was told where to sit. Then, formal introductions were made.

"This is Miss Charlotte." Maribelle pointed to a Madame Alexander Doll that looked remarkably like her including sporting a white apron over a blue dress. Then, Addy was introduced to Mary Catherine Louisa March, Miss Piggy, Prickly Puss, and a host of others.

Addy balanced herself on a tiny chair, hoping like hell it'd hold.

"Daddy has tea with me sometimes." She lifted a teapot and poured her "tea." "You can come, too."

"Thank you." She lifted the tiny plastic cup to her lips and pretended to take a sip.

A low chatter grew downstairs. The party must have begun, though Maribelle didn't seem to notice. Instead, the little girl had a *lot* to say.

For long minutes, Addy drank her pretend tea and Maribelle filled her in on how Prickly Puss got her name. The pink elephant fell into a rosebush after asking Maribelle to get closer so she could smell them. Then Maribelle was *attacked*, her exact words, by the rosebush.

Mary Catherine Louisa March were all her favorite names. And her doll—a blond, more realistic-sized version of Barbie—deserved having all the best names. In fact, the doll demanded it.

Miss Charlotte was a big bully who was always telling Miss Piggy what to do, but Miss Piggy was having none of it. The two were "frem-en-emies."

Forget the stupid *Genius* books and their teachings. His little girl didn't need them. She was not only smart, she had imagination galore.

"Maybe they'll be real friends someday," Addy said. "Hey, I don't suppose you have your own bathroom up here." Despite the fact she had been drinking air, Addy had to pee.

Maribelle's tiny brows furrowed. "Of course I do."

Of course, she did.

Addie rose and shook out her hips. Sitting in a chair that even Prickly Puss had trouble staying in proved to be a challenge. "I'll be right back."

"Don't forget to wash your hands."

"Oh, I never forget that." Especially not in this house.

Addie stopped in the doorway. "Wow. Fancy." But it would be with a marble sink and matching marble footstool pulled up so Maribelle could reach it. Addy did her business, and when she returned, the tea-table was abandoned, at least of anything human.

"Maribelle? Are we playing hide and seek now?" No tell-tale giggle rang in the air. Maribelle had probably learned to hide very well. Addy would have to figure out what was up with her deep aversion to strangers. Normal shyness was one thing; fear of all new people told a completely different story.

If only Addy hadn't ended her subscription to *Celebrity* magazine last year—or her sister remembered to tell her things—she'd have learned more about this little girl. Like the fact he had Maribelle *at all,* and with a former client: *the* Kate Tremont, the face of a designer whose name Addy could never pronounce. Ash would be with someone like her. Someone whose legs were always shaved even if running a razor over so much human real estate must take hours.

At least her famous mother kept Maribelle out of the paparazzis' eye given how little she found online about her that afternoon. Maybe Ash was here to hide Maribelle away from the celebrity lifestyle. Being recognized everywhere you go, chased and *oo-ed* and *ah-ed* over every second of the day couldn't be much fun—certainly not for a six-year-old.

"Maribelle? Where are you?" She wasn't in her closet, under her bed, or in the huge, creepy armoire that housed a bunch of musty-smelling quilts. Addy deserved a medal for even checking there.

It finally dawned on her. Maribelle wasn't anywhere in the room. Great. One hour on the job and she'd lost the genius child.

Addy lifted her arms, let them slap to her sides. "You didn't go downstairs, Maribelle, right?"

She sucked in a long breath. "Crap. You went downstairs, didn't you?" To sneak a cupcake in her magic cloak, no doubt.

Well, the gig was nice while it lasted.

4

Ash lifted Maribelle into his arms. "What are you doing down here? Everything okay?"

When she tumbled into the room and made a beeline for him, he was sure she'd gotten scared about something—enough to brave a room full of new adults.

"Smell, Daddy. It my magic oil." She stuck her arm in front of his face.

"Mmm, I can smell it." Lavender? He bumped his nose against hers.

Adelaide appeared next to them. His gaze locked on her. "Miss Bloom." She had one job. One. He set Maribelle down, who immediately clung to his leg.

A smile formed on her face. "Hi. Queen Maribelle, I think our tea is getting cold."

Maribelle slipped her hand into Addy's. "But I had to have Daddy smell my magic oil."

He cocked an eyebrow. "Magic, huh?"

Addy shrugged lightly. "Imagination is good for genius kids, right?" Her lips stretched wider.

Just what he thought. She was used to getting out of any number of sticky situations with her smile.

"Something going on I need to know about?" If that nanny did anything to scare his daughter…

"Oh, no," Adelaide tittered. "She… slipped out."

A female squeal sent a chill up his spine. "Adelaide Bloom. Imagine seeing you here."

The nanny's face hardened. His likely did, as well.

The room was too small already, but it shrank considerably when Sally Albrecchio inched closer to him. She was the kind of woman that reminded him why he didn't date. Sharp perfume invaded his space. Long, pink nails tapped against a champagne flute marred with a lip print. She was critical to getting Maribelle settled at the Moorsville Girls Academy, however.

"Hi, Sally." Adelaide drew Maribelle closer. "What are you doing here?"

She scoffed. "I'm here to welcome our new Moorsvillian to town." She placed her arm on his. "Mr. Scott, what a beautiful little girl you have." Sally gave Maribelle a slight nod. "Hello, sweetheart."

Maribelle gave her a shy smile. "You have big lips."

"Maribelle." His girl knew better than that.

His little girl flapped her hands for Adelaide to get closer. "Addy." The nanny bent at the waist and Maribelle whispered loud enough for anyone in the room to hear. "The magic cloak works. The magic oil, too."

What on earth was this woman telling his daughter? Lord knows what else went on in the one hour the nanny and his daughter were upstairs. He could deal with one night. Then again, look what one night produced—Maribelle. He wasn't sorry for that one. She was the only good in his life right now.

Adelaide straightened. "You are so brave."

"Magic?" Sally swirled her glass of Prosecco. "I see you're up to your old tricks, Addy."

So, Adelaide and Sally had a history. It was a small-town, after all.

"Oh, no tricks. Just a little lavender." Adelaide gazed down at Maribelle. "And it *is* magic."

He gestured to the hallway. "Adelaide, why don't you take Maribelle back upstairs?"

The nanny began to lead Maribelle away when the mayor, Pat Townsend, sidled up to Adelaide and put his arm around her. "I agree on the lavender. Works like a charm. Hello, Addy. So wonderful to see you here." He gave her a big kiss on the cheek, and her signature smile blossomed once more on her face. "I knew you were a smart man, Mr. Scott. Our Addy here is a legend."

She flushed.

"Is that right?" He lifted his near-empty tumbler to a woman in a black apron holding a tray. He needed another stiff one if he was to get through any more small talk.

"Oh, I'd say Addy is a legend alright." Sally took a sip of her drink and bent her head toward him. "Adelaide has… unique ideas around childcare. But I went to the Moorsville Girls Academy, and as a board member, I can assure you we pride ourselves on taking a traditional approach. We'll take care of Maribelle for you. No magic oil required." She stared hard at Adelaide, who didn't flinch.

Adelaide lifted her chin. "I choose what's best for the situation at hand. So, you're on the school's board now?"

"Of course. And you're a… nanny. Still."

Small towns and their hidden stories. Sally seemed quite a bit older than Adelaide, but it didn't take Sherlock Holmes to see she and this woman had quite a past. It didn't matter what so long as it didn't impact his child, and he wouldn't be around enough to need to know more. "Adelaide, why don't you take Maribelle back upstairs?"

Sally squared herself to him. "I can't tell you how pleased we are to welcome Maribelle to the school. To think we'll have such an esteemed alumna." The woman was nearly breathless —or perhaps her breath was bated. Fundraising boards could smell a dollar a mile away. "We will take very good care of her."

The woman beamed down at Maribelle, whose brows pinched together. *Dammit.* He hadn't had time to prepare her for the term yet or even mention the school.

Maribelle peered up at him. "But Addy takes care of me."

Strange. His little girl didn't take to people easily.

Adelaide swiped hair off her forehead. "Time for bed, Maribelle. I have stories to tell you."

"But I have six minutes. Right, Daddy?" Her little pout was going to kill him one day.

O'Connor sidled up to them, of course. "Yes, join our little party." He held out his hand to Adelaide, who returned his handshake. "I'm Chief O'Connor—"

"Fire chief?" Maribelle blinked at him.

He chuckled. "Oh, no. Public relations. My parents had a funny sense of humor with my name. But please, stay." O'Connor inclined his head toward Ash and lowered his voice. "It'll be good for people to see you with the child and how you hired a local."

"No." He wouldn't have Maribelle fawned over and fondled by strangers. "Nanny? Bed, please." He'd agreed to meet the local leaders—chamber head, mayor, Moorsville Girls Academy board members, and other small-town dignitaries to quell any budding gossip about their presence, but he'd not subject Maribelle to inspection.

"Ad-e-laide. Bloom." A guy in a plaid jacket, of all things, was next to join the growing knot of people around him and his daughter. "You still watching kids? Mr. Scott, you got yourself a find with this one."

Jesus Christ. This woman was like the town magnet. "So I hear."

Adelaide's face stretched wide. "Hi, Mr. Jameson."

The guy lifted his glass and pointed a finger at him. "A true legend in this town. Sorted my kids right out."

Adelaide pulled Maribelle closer to her by the shoulders, thank God. The cluster was growing around them, and a meltdown could start at any point. He reached for her, but she drew closer to the nanny.

"How is Clementine?" Adelaide asked Jameson. "And Jacob? Heard he made the little league team."

"Sure did. Mr. Scott, Adelaide here coached my Jacob right to victory on that one."

He pursed his lips and nodded to signal the man's news was the most important of the night. It wasn't, but the man also was on the board of the Moorsville Girls Academy, and a good impression had to be made.

"Jacob is naturally gifted." Adelaide nodded once. "Please, give them my best."

"Addy." Maribelle threw her arms up at her—a move he'd never seen her do with anyone but him.

After lifting her into her arms, Maribelle dropped her head to Addy's shoulder. "Addy is my nanny now."

"You can be mine," a round-faced man who was clearly in his cups whispered over her other shoulder.

Adelaide startled and wrinkled her nose. "Hi, Kip." She jostled Maribelle into a better position. "Six minutes are up, Queen Maribelle." She spun away from the interloper.

"Hey where you going, Addy? I wanted to see how you were."

Ash had no idea who this man was, but his red nose could

stick itself elsewhere. Clearly, Ash had to break this knot of humanity that had formed around them.

"Excuse us." He led Adelaide out by the elbow to the hallway. "Maribelle…"

He took his girl from Adelaide's arms and kissed Maribelle on her forehead. "Why don't you head on upstairs? I'm going to have a minute with Adelaide here. Can you head up by yourself?"

"Sure, Daddy. I have the magic cloak."

He set her down and Maribelle skipped up the stairs. To have the resiliency of a six-year-old…

He turned to his one-night-only babysitter.

"I'm really sorry she came down. I had to pee and…"

He held up his hand, silencing her words. "It's fine. It seems you know quite a few people in this town."

"Yeah, sorry." She waved her hand toward the library behind them. "But I'm not trying to stick out or anything. I'm trying to blend in. I swear."

What a strange thing to say. "Fine, fine." He knew enough about this woman that stopping her gush of words early and often was necessary.

"I mean I won't bring any trouble to you."

Great. There was a significant story, wasn't there? He'd moved himself and his daughter from New York to get away from complexities, not enter new ones. "The minute someone says they won't bring trouble, it means they have in the past."

"Well, it's never been my fault. Does that count?"

He cocked his head. "You wouldn't believe the excuses I've heard. I'm an attorney."

Her blue-gray eyes grew wide. "I'll bet you've heard everything."

"You could say that." This woman's justifications, however, did not interest him. "Now, about the Moorsville

Girls Academy. Maribelle has yet to learn of her enrollment —until tonight."

"And Sally let the cat out of the bag. She's good that way."

"I'm sure Maribelle will question you. Don't go into it with her."

"Gotcha. Haven't sprung it on her yet. I got you covered." She winked, an uncomfortable shock traveling up his spine. This woman's casual air was damned unnerving.

"Springing things on my daughter is not how I would characterize it."

She ran her fingers over her lips in an imaginary zipper motion. "My lips are zipped."

He doubted that. He moved to turn away but, as usual, she had more to say.

"I promise you she'll probably love it there despite Sally's whole traditional thing."

"There is nothing wrong with tradition." His mother was an exemplary example of what the school could produce, though why she and his father deemed to settle in this nothing town he'd never understand. Either one of them could have done anything. Been anyone. Maribelle would not suffer a small town beyond a few years at the school. She'd get a stellar education, fall from the gossip rag's interest, and move on—like he would.

Stevens appeared behind him. "Mr. Scott, I'm so sorry to interrupt, but Mrs. Dexter is here for you. In your office."

Excellent. "Let O'Connor know I'll be back in a minute. Got called away on business." He turned to Adelaide. "Attend to Maribelle, please? Good night, Miss Bloom."

He spun on his heel and strode across the foyer to his makeshift office. He found one very red-faced Mrs. Dexter twisting her hands together, standing before his desk.

"Mr. Scott." She rushed forward. "I am so sorry to break

into your party, but I wanted to give you the news right away in person."

"You have good news for me?"

"I'm afraid not."

He knew what was coming next.

The woman shifted on her low heels. "We pride ourselves on placing the best people with you, and Adelaide—"

He raised his hand to slice her words short. "You didn't find any other nannies for me, did you, Mrs. Dexter?"

"I tried. I really did, but Adelaide—"

"I can stay." Adelaide appeared in the doorway like a ghost —or a stealth bomber.

"Aren't you supposed to be upstairs watching my daughter?"

"On my way. I can even spend the night tonight. I brought an overnight bag. I find it's wise to always be prepared and—"

For the second—hundredth?—time that night, he raised his hand to stop unwanted words. And as an attorney, he thought he used a lot, but this woman took talking to a new level. "You seem quite popular, Adelaide. I am sure you can find another job elsewhere."

Her hometown acclaim was the thing that didn't sit well with him. She seemed to be popular alright—with the men. The women? Not so much. Beautiful women often suffered that kind of attention dichotomy, which was another thing he should not be noticing about this woman. A pretty face usually brought trouble, and he'd moved to Moorsville to avoid any more scandal centering around females.

Maribelle threw herself against his legs. "Yay. Addy can stay!" So, she'd snuck inside.

He was officially surrounded. Outnumbered. Three against one.

Mrs. Dexter who couldn't seem to do her job. A country

nanny that had some sort of backstory he shouldn't be interested in but now might have to ferret out to ensure it didn't negatively affect Maribelle. And now, his little girl who looked at him with her huge blue eyes and lethal pout… like her mother's.

Her eyes blinked up at him.

Fuck him. The littlest one in the room probably had the most power here because he was going to end up hiring Adelaide Bloom, wasn't he?

"Mrs. Dexter, is this a temporary glitch or permanent? Truth, please."

"Everyone is placed. Except…" She eyed Adelaide, who was grinning from ear to ear. No one could smile that much and not suffer TMJ.

He sighed. Practically Perfect Nannies vetted their au pairs very well—at least, that had been his experience this past year with its New York office, especially after the first fiasco hiring someone not with a reputable agency. He had no reason to believe the woman standing before him right now was any different, small-town backstory or not. Most of the people across the hallway seemed to like her, even though Ms. Albrecchio most definitely didn't. He'd find out more about that obvious rivalry on his own. In the meantime, he was stuck.

He looked over at Adelaide.

Her smile dropped. Now she understood his stare?

She swallowed. "I won't let you down."

What choice did he have? "You can stay the week. On probation. Then we'll see." She'd be out on her pert behind if she proved too much trouble. "Tomorrow morning. My office. We'll discuss things then."

Maribelle jumped up and down, squeezing his legs "You are the best daddy ever."

If only that was true, though his little girl's eyes were

shining with something other than tears for the first time in months. He'd take it because *her* smile was all that mattered.

Mrs. Dexter rushed up to him. "I think you'll be quite pleased with Adelaide. She's a legend."

"So I hear." Adelaide was likely the town beauty queen or long-ago head cheerleader who stole some other girl's boyfriend. It had to be something simple like that. God, let it be something simple like that.

Adelaide laughed. "Well, legend might be stretching it."

"Actually, it's not." Mrs. Dexter raised her eyebrows in the girl's direction.

He rubbed his forehead. With any luck, there'd be a New York woman who was dying to land in a small town. Why did he know there was no such thing? The last one he'd tried to import couldn't get on a flight back fast enough.

At least Adelaide seemed versed in the Moorsville Girls Academy—and he was out of time to find someone else to help Maribelle get ready for it. They only had a few weeks left.

And perhaps he was being too sensitive, too harsh without having all the facts about her. Perhaps he'd been in New York too long. Or the year of being hounded by gossip and scandal had permanently eroded his ability to trust anyone.

Truthfully, how much harm could Adelaide do really?

5

Ash couldn't catch a break. "What do you mean they refuse to teleconference?"

"They want an in-person." Stevens clutched the clipboard she never parted from close to her chest. "This afternoon."

"Less than six hours' notice and they want me to get to New York. It's not like there's an hourly shuttle like from DC or Philly. Jesus." Why hadn't he moved to a new city, one within striking distance of New York at least? Forgo this hometown nonsense altogether?

This meeting development meant one of two things. The opposition was buying time to gather new evidence to swing a win at a trial, or the opposing counsel was swinging his dick around and wanted the great Ashton Scott to grovel.

Ash didn't grovel. Ever.

"You can catch the flight I'm taking back." O'Connor lazily sipped his coffee. The man had crashed in a guest bedroom last night and was now taking up too much space in his office.

Ash rubbed his forehead. "Next time, remember to bring

in a private jet. Commercial in and out of this place is ridiculous."

"It's not so bad here." O'Connor yawned. "Except quiet as hell. Couldn't sleep for shit. Need the traffic white noise from New York, I guess."

Ash, on the other hand, had been sleeping like the dead for the first time in twelve years. Something was off about this place.

Damn. He'd had a decent morning before this summons to New York. He'd got in a brain-cleansing seven-mile run. Not a single photographer jumped out at him. And when he returned? All remnants of last night's shindig had been removed from the library.

Of course, as soon as he arrived in his office, he came face to face with an email from Mrs. Dexter. She'd sent a contract and an outline of Adelaide Bloom's accomplishments.

Twenty-seven families. High ratings for happy children. Works well under strict supervision. Red flag there. No mention of any scandals, but would they have included it? Hardly.

Ash stuffed papers into a satchel, cursing under his breath to let off some steam. Maybe he'd stop at the Practically Perfect Nannies agency in New York, find some elderly woman who'd love to have her last gig in a sleepy little North Carolina town.

O'Connor eyed him. "I know what you're thinking. You're doing good, Ash. It's a smart move to be here. Believe me. You're making it look like you're doing everything for the little kid."

He *was* doing everything for his little kid. "Maribelle."

Amazing how his hometown was voted as one of the most idyllic places to raise a child or some shit. Bonus point that it also had a great girl's academy with a 99 percent college placement history with one of the big six universities.

He'd spend a year here to slowly transition Maribelle to a boarding situation during the week. Then he'd get his ass back to New York where things made sense for the weekdays and come home on weekends. It could work. That is if the gossip rags left him alone.

O'Connor slapped the chair arms and rose. "Ya' know, it would help a lot if you got a wife. People love that, 'I moved for love,' crap. 'Prodigal son returns home and charms the locals,' stuff."

He had moved for love—a little girl's. As for his move, it was temporary as all things are.

O'Connor continued to sip from a coffee mug. "Surely, you can find a woman here. I gotta say, Moorsville's got some lookers. Your nanny is something."

He scoffed. This man was supposed to keep him out of the headlines, not hand him an idea that'd land him on the front page of some scandal sheet.

The man continued to eye him. "Don't tell me you didn't notice her. Everyone else last night did."

"Women don't interest me."

O'Connor howled heartily. "Since when? But good deal on hiring her, especially during last night's party. It's good for the locals to see you hire local."

"Maribelle seems to like her." His daughter would like any woman at this point. His heart panged like a tin drum. Losing her mother at age five? That would be the last time his little girl felt loss if he had anything to do with it.

He scrubbed his chin. "Listen, I've got to go say goodbye to Maribelle. Give me a few minutes."

He also had to talk to Adelaide. If he had to leave for a full day—maybe overnight because Lord knew what flight schedule led back here—he'd make sure the woman had some ground rules. *His* rules.

O'Connor buttoned his jacket. "I'll pull my rental around. Outside in thirty?"

"Less than." How hard could it be to lay down some ground rules with a nanny?

He took the steps leading to the second floor two at a time and headed toward the music. "Dancing Queen" by ABBA was on full blast.

He turned the corner and stopped short in the doorway of Maribelle's room.

She and Adelaide stood in front of the floor-length mirror in the far corner. His little girl wore a yellow dress ten times too large for her. He recognized the gown immediately and swallowed. His body couldn't seem to move.

It was the dress Kate wore the night she'd met him. Some awards dinner.

The color of the dress, a bright spot of sunshine, had stood out in the sea of black dresses. It had highlighted her dark hair and skin. It made him think of all those Black-Eyed Susan daisies his mother had insisted on planting in the backyard garden.

Kate had walked right up to him. Asked him about a contract clause. Shocked him with the intelligence of her question.

She'd mesmerized him—for one night. And it was as long as their connection could last. They'd parted the next morning as friends. He'd thought they were friends anyway. Friends who lost touch until he heard the news of her death and a day later got the call summoning him to the will reading where he was introduced to his daughter.

Fuck, his heart squeezed remembering the first time he looked into Maribelle's red-rimmed eyes—his eyes. He knew right away she was his. She then did the strangest thing. She'd run up to him, tilted her head back, and asked, "You're my daddy, aren't you?"

He was—and had been from that second on.

He leaned against the door jamb.

Maribelle grabbed handfuls of the fabric and swished and twisted it. Where on earth had she gotten the dress?

He was unable to take his eyes off her. She really did look like Kate. An overwhelming urge to wrap her in his arms and never let another soul get within a mile of her rushed through his whole body.

Maybe he had done the right thing, bringing her here. His brain was racked with ways he could get out of this bullshit meeting that would take him back to Manhattan. Nothing came up because, truth was, he had to win this case. One more loss this year and his firm would give him the final boot. They barely tolerated him living states away, though they loved no longer having paparazzi parked outside head-quarters every day.

"Fashion show!" Adelaide beamed at him in the mirror. "What do you think?"

Maribelle turned and rushed toward him in a rustle of chiffon. Mercifully, Adelaide reached for her phone, and the music dimmed.

Maribelle nearly tripped, and he caught her and lifted her up in his arms. "My, aren't you beautiful."

"It was Mama's. It was her favorite and she let me have it in my dress-up box." Tears threatened in her eyes.

The dress had been Kate's favorite? A wave of something unpleasant—nostalgia? melancholy? regret?—threatened to sneak under his skin. Maybe he should have stayed in touch with her. To think he could have known Maribelle her entire life and not five years into it.

Stop. He shook off the brief moment of sentimentality. He had no time for it.

"Fit for a queen," he added quickly and brushed Maribelle's hair from her forehead. "I came to tell you I have to go away on a work trip."

"Noooo." *That pout.*

"Miss Bloom is going to take care of you." He eyed Adelaide and hoped his presumption she could stay evenings as well as daytimes wasn't met with horror.

Rather, Adelaide clapped her hands. "Sleepover!"

Maribelle's forehead smoothed and her smile was back. "She can stay in my room, Daddy."

He set Maribelle on her feet. "I think she might enjoy a room of her own." His gaze lifted to the woman. "Take any bedroom on this floor." He cocked his head toward the entrance. "Can we talk for a minute?"

She nodded once.

He led Maribelle back into the room. "I'll be back to say goodbye, I promise. And I won't be gone long."

She dragged the dress back to the mirror and picked up one of her dolls. "Okay. I have the magic cape that matches my dress."

The reality of Maribelle's situation mentally slapped his forehead as if saying, "Wake up, already." Magic anything wasn't going to help his daughter, and it was time Adelaide learned why. Her imaginative ways to calm kids might work for the children of Moorsville, but Maribelle's life had been nothing like the kids who grew up here.

They stepped out together into the hallway. "My office." He thought better there.

He also needed Maribelle out of earshot. It was time to fill Adelaide in on some things. The question was how much to tell her.

Adelaide took the club chair in front of Ash's desk. She took a quick second to glance around the office, something she didn't have time for the other day. It was spacious since it once was the front parlor. Fireplace behind his chair. A curio cabinet in the corner. Her heart pinged a little at seeing two Hummel figurines Mrs. Scott loved. Addy had dusted those eons ago.

Ash cleared his throat, lifted his blue eyes her way. Worry lines creased his forehead.

"Are you okay?" she asked.

His face stilled, and all emotion in his face faded as if a cloud had drifted overhead and blocked the sun. He didn't want her to know what he thought.

Oh, criminy, had Sally called him? Fed him a lot of horse poop?

He sighed heavily. "I'm fine. Can you stay nights? I'll pay overtime, of course."

Okay, whatever Sally might have said clearly wasn't the worst of it. He wouldn't ask her to stay if Sally had told him everything. "Absolutely."

He finally dropped himself into his chair, leaned back, assessed her. "I'm leaving for New York."

"Leaving. Already?" Why was her heart doing a squeezy thing? It's because she just got this job, that was all. She didn't want to lose it.

"Possibly overnight."

"Oh, temporarily." Her breath returned to her lungs, which was strange it'd vanished at all.

He steepled his hands. "While I'm gone, I expect Maribelle to adhere to her schedule. We also have some simple house rules for you to follow."

"Can't wait to hear them." She tried to sound supportive, but by the way his blue eyes fired, she had to swallow down a lump in her throat. His freezy face was good—and kinda hot.

No wonder all the women last night practically drooled all over his suit, especially Sally. But then, women always had that reaction to him, including her.

"Bedtime is strictly at 7:30 p.m. She often needs help falling asleep. Sit with her."

Oh, he didn't want to leave his daughter. Her jaw ached at how sweet that was. There was little in life more endearing than a dad worrying about his girl, especially from someone she'd never expect would actually care about anything other than himself.

Judgey of her, but she had evidence, even if it was fourteen years ago.

"You already have her mealtime schedule. You and Maribelle are not to leave the property without permission. You will have no guests—especially boys."

A horse laugh erupted from her throat. But she quickly swallowed it down. *Crap.* Sally *had* said something to him.

His chair thunked to upright. "Something funny?"

"I'm 29 years old. I don't really have boys around." At least, not in years.

"Semantics. No people of the male—or female—persuasion that are not a member of my staff on the premises. You seem to know a lot of people here in town. I don't want any of them getting the wrong idea like that man at the party."

She was unable to tamp down a laugh. "Kip? Oh, he's harmless. He's been after me for years."

Okay, wrong thing to say given the way his eyes flamed like a dragon lived inside him. The man's eyes really were a-maz-ing. It was too bad they sat in a face so grumbly. "I'm single so…"

"Your marital status is of no concern. Just make sure he doesn't *get you*. Not in this house."

In that one instant, she was fifteen again. Like she'd once again rounded the corner, ran into him, and looked into those incredible eyes as his hands wrapped around her biceps.

But then he'd dashed any hope she existed on any plane he might live on. How she wasn't destined for anything.

She straightened her spine, remembering herself. "I'm not that easy."

"That's not what I meant." He raised his hand.

"What then?"

"Look, I apologize. Honestly, we shouldn't even be having this conversation. It's…"

"I understand you're under a lot of stress and strain." Never mind his six-year-old who cried this morning in her closet suddenly wanting her mother—until Addy had found that dress and said they should play dress up.

"I'm fine." He shot to standing and ran his hand through his hair as if irritated.

Okay, her tone of voice was completely lost on this man. "You keep saying that but—"

His blue fiery eyes sliced to her. "Do you always talk to your bosses this way? So directly?"

She snapped her lips shut. She was on a probationary period after all.

He scrubbed his hair again and began to pace behind his desk. "I'm concerned about Maribelle being alone in this house."

"She's not alone. She has me. What can I say to make you feel better about that?" Addy was used to having to prove herself, so why not to Ashton Scott?

"Follow my rules."

He kept saying that, too. She nodded, and his shoulders relaxed. Man, they could not be more opposite. He clearly loved regulations and instructions. As for her? One shouldn't ever fall in love with something meant to shoehorn people into little boxes.

"Now, about Maribelle. As you have already surmised…"

The fact he used the word "surmised" almost raised another snigger from her, but she did a reasonable job of redirecting it. He didn't seem appreciative of lightness, either. Then again, he was leaving his daughter who hid in closets and "fortressed."

"Maribelle starts at the Academy on September tenth. She's never been to a school—"

"Never? Oh, sorry. Go ahead."

He took in a measured breath as if steeling himself. "She's had private tutors and playdates with other children but never a classroom setting."

"And first grade means sitting in a classroom for long hours at a time, adhering to a schedule. I get where you're going." Finally, they had something in common. "Why anyone makes a bunch of little kids try to sit still, I'll never know."

"She is very well prepared academically, but it's impera-tive she stick to a schedule now."

"And get her ready for her first day. The first day is every-thing." She was so on top of this. He didn't need to worry. "What are we getting for her backpack? And the outfit? There's the picture in the morning—"

"Miss Bloom."

His bark made her startle.

"My apologies. I'm in a bit of a hurry." He leveled his gaze on her. "The Moorsville Academy has uniforms."

"Of course, but then it will be all about the hair ribbon." She tapped a finger to her lips. Maribelle would look stun-ning in a yellow ribbon. "I'm thinking yellow. It's her favorite color, and that dress looked so good on her, didn't it?"

His jaw tensed and he nodded once. Then his Adam's apple bobbed, but not in an uncertain way. More like he was holding something big in. Maybe the dragon fire she'd seen earlier.

What had she said? "Didn't you like it?"

"It was her mother's dress."

Okay, now all the air truly was gone from her lungs. She wasn't a stupid person, so why hadn't she thought of that? She should have. How else did a six-year-old have a trunk full of designer clothes if not from her supermodel mother? Or—and this is where her mind had gone—they came from women whose dresses ended up puddled at their feet while Ash divested them of the clothing.

Twenty-four hours into her new job and she'd had an epic fail. This man lost someone he cared about. He had a child with her. Adelaide had been snippy and so... well, herself. "I'm sorry. I didn't know." Could she sound any more lame?

"It's fine." There was that word again. He pinched the bridge of his nose, which he also did a lot.

She could fix this. "What do you need?"

He blinked at her. "*I* don't need anything."

She sent a silent prayer up to the almighty goddesses he didn't have mind-reading capability for her earlier admiring thoughts about him. This was way more important. "I mean what can I do to assure you that Maribelle is going to be fine? With me."

He leveled his gaze on her. "Follow the book. The rules. Her schedule." He reached over to a stack of books and handed her the top one. "Should you need a reference manual..."

She glanced down at the book. "*The Genius Child Guide to Starting First Grade.*" She studied the back. "Shaping tomorrow's citizens. Inspiring the creative brain center. Centering the child for accelerated learning. Personalized learning pathways igniting..." She looked up at him. Man, this guy was smokin', but he was going to be toast if he thought this book was going to help him with Maribelle.

Igniting a six-year-old didn't require a manual. They came pre-lit.

"Um… about this…" She waved the book.

"Need an interpretation?"

Of the bull caca she was handed? No. She shook her head.

"Now, there's more to tell you, but," he glanced down at his watch, "I'm afraid I'm out of time. When I get back, I'll fill you in, but promise me. No leaving without permission. No outsiders. We had a few scares in New York, so this is imperative."

He was fearful of something. It was so evident. She nodded. "Of course."

He huffed out a breath as if relieved. "Good. Now, if you'll excuse me, I'm going to say goodbye to Maribelle and then catch a plane."

He gestured for her to walk out. She hugged the useless book to her chest and followed him out into the foyer. Maybe the press of the hardback would hold all the words inside her that wanted to erupt.

"Here is a credit card and my card with my cell phone number on it. I expect updates on Maribelle." He held them back when she reached for them. "Use them wisely. Anything you need for her." He then handed them to her. "Other than that, go to Stevens."

The credit card was thick metal. Platinum-looking. His business card was equally weighty. "Wow. I could pop some doors open with this thing. Not that I would, of course."

He turned at the first step of the staircase. "Oh, and Miss Bloom. You're not to utter a word about what you hear or see here. I work hard to protect our privacy. I realize your agency has an NDA built into its contract, but I expect you to exceed its stipulations for discretion."

"I'm glad you have rules, Mr. Scott. Not everyone does." She supposed some rules were okay, even if he did talk like a legal textbook. "You had great parents, and it shows." And she was pretty sure they didn't consult *The Genius Child Guide*.

He scoffed. "I had great nannies. Please, try to be a great one for my daughter's sake."

"Yes, sir. No sugar. Don't get dirty. No strangers. Inspire the creative brain center and ignite a personalized learning pathway."

Ash smirked and shook his head. He then turned and left her in the alcove.

The Exalted One didn't believe she could do it, did he? She was made for—she checked the back of the book again—shaping, inspiring, centering, and most definitely *personalizing*. And she knew exactly how to start.

Maribelle was going to get a little dirty, though.

6

———

Someone around the conference table cleared their throat. Ash lifted his head from his phone.

Saunders smiled over at him. "Need a break? Again?"

"Do you?" He gave the guy a half-smile back—which was more than the studio's attorney deserved.

"No, it's just…" He waved his hand and glanced down at the phone in Ash's hand—the phone that hadn't stopped buzzing with incoming texts all afternoon from *that nanny.*

First, there were simple questions, asking if it was okay for them to walk all over the property. Easy. He typed back his usual response with a "Y." Any sane person would take that as a "Yes." Adelaide Bloom required confirmation that Y stood for yes, which was another freaking text back to her

Then, the pictures began to roll in.

Maribelle with her dolls,

Maribelle running around the backyard barefoot. Her dress floating in the wind. Leaves in her hair.

Maribelle chin deep in a tub with bubbles all around her —and five of her dolls. The caption to that one read, "Soaking off the day."

He glanced one more time at his phone to gall the guy.

<<The Pink or the Yellow?>>

Two pictures of ribbons in Maribelle's hair followed. He quickly tapped out a reply. Took his time doing it, too. Let Saunders wait.

<<Later for further questions.>>

Hell, everything she'd asked this afternoon could have waited. He was glad for updates but didn't expect one every five minutes.

He set his phone face down on the table and cleared his throat. "Saunders, if you're going to breach a contract for Miss Winston at least show some imagination." Not willing to pay the actress her cut for the film because it went straight to streaming over theatre? Not on his watch.

"Forgot to read the fine print, did we?" The dick attorney was swinging his man organ around pretty well today.

"You and I both know there is nothing there to call for this insanity."

"Let's talk more tomorrow." The guy yawned. "These talks demand a bit more consideration. Unless you have to get back to that little town of yours."

"One more day won't change our stance." But, yeah, he was likely spending the night here. He could ill afford to lose this case. It was his ticket back to the good graces of the celebrities who lived and breathed Manhattan. His clients brought in the most revenue to his firm—or, they had.

His phone buzzed again. Dammit, he forgot to take off the vibration. Probably another question, such as asking if "further questions" meant "all questions." He should have administered a drug test before hiring this woman.

He spent another forty-five minutes going back and forth with Saunders until everyone agreed they'd pick up again the next day. He did a reasonable job ignoring his phone until he got to his apartment and had some space.

He loosened his tie, grabbed a beer from the refrigerator, and settled himself in the chair by the window overlooking the river. The beer left a cool trail down his throat, nearly raw from choking back retorts all day.

His apartment didn't smell right. Like dust but also furniture polish. He'd kept up his weekly maid service despite the fact he was here less and less each week.

He scrolled through the pictures from the day.

One of them caught his eye. The yellow ribbon looked better on Maribelle than the pink. It was an opinion he would have never had a year ago.

His daughter truly was gorgeous like her mother. A thick cloud filled his insides at the thought of Kate being gone. They barely knew each other, and certainly, one night together wasn't enough to fall in love, not even close, but he wished she was here. His little girl didn't deserve to grow up motherless.

He massaged the back of his neck. Being back in New York should have felt better than it did. Instead, all day, a hollow pit in his stomach grew where once a fire raged. Energy used to course through his veins when facing opposing counsel. Hell, even just walking the crowded streets, yelling out an order at the Kramstoke Deli around the corner from his office, hailing a cab. Now, it reminded him how little he recognized his life anymore.

His thumb swiped again and again, drinking in the

pictures of his daughter. He'd never regret doing what was best for her. She'd do better away from the city mayhem. He'd never allow her to be turned into an object of fascination like her mother—hounded, stalked.

As for him? His life had to be put on hold.

His gaze locked on the final picture. Maribelle tucked in bed with a huge grin on her face, holding the Velveteen Rabbit. He loved that book as a kid.

<<Want to Facetime for storytime?>>

Thoughtful of Adelaide to think of having him join them. If only this country nanny wasn't so… loud. Not in volume but in sucking all the oxygen out of every space she entered. Maybe that's why she was still single. Anyone who looked like her, loved kids? Should have had a few offers to walk down the dreaded wedding aisle by now or already been married with six kids running around her.

He dialed the nanny's number.

"Hi." Her voice was low and hushed. "She just got to sleep."

"Ah, too late for *The Velveteen Rabbit*."

The muffled sound of a door closing sounded in his ear. "Do you want me to wake her up? I can, though I would not advise it."

"No, that's okay. Thank you for the pictures." His voice rasped, so he took another swig of beer. "But you don't have to send me one every five minutes. A few updates are fine."

"She wanted me to send you all of them."

"She did?" He wondered if his own parents would have used such technology to stay in touch with him. He laughed internally at himself. Of course, they wouldn't have. Distance was the middle name of his childhood.

"Don't tell her, but I didn't send all the photos we took. It's amazing you have your own monkey bars out back. I don't remember those. She did at least ten somersaults on them, and wouldn't you know it? I didn't have my phone on video. My bad."

His lips released the edge of the beer bottle. "You let Maribelle play on those disgusting things? You wiped them down? Checked the security of the structure?"

"You mean the steel pipes that have been there for forty years that can withstand a hurricane? I promise to get out the Clorox wipes next time."

He was overdoing it. "New York makes me tense."

"I'll bet. Everything going okay up there?"

"The same. Yet not." His chest began to ache with a need to be with his little girl—her smiles, her energy. "How is she? We haven't been apart much since…" Shit, he didn't even want to say it. It'd just start a conversation that needed to be had in person.

"She's great. We're over here inspiring her creative brain center. Though, I gotta tell you, she could teach me a thing or two."

"Oh, yeah?"

"The girl's got an eye for color. She dressed me this morning."

He chuckled.

"You laugh, but seriously, I've never looked so good."

He put her on speakerphone and scrolled through the pictures until he found the one again of Adelaide next to the bathtub. He widened it. The woman had pretty eyes, and her top did bring out the blue in them. The T-shirt also was wet, revealing her bra. What the hell was he doing? He set his phone down.

Adelaide cleared her throat. "Speaking of which… mind if I break the seal on the credit card and get her some play clothes? I couldn't find a single pair of leggings."

"Whatever she needs. And the yellow ribbon looks better."

"Told ya.'"

He scoffed. "Don't let it go to your head. Good night, Miss Bloom."

"Good night, *Mr. Scott*." There was a tease in her voice. It didn't bother him even though it should have.

He killed the call and laid the phone face down on the table. He wished like hell he'd made more time before having to return to New York, had told Adelaide more about why they had to leave New York. About all the people wanting a piece of his daughter.

Like those fuckers would ever get the chance. Over his stone-cold dead body.

He picked up his phone and flipped through the day's pictures once more. He was getting Maribelle a German shepherd puppy for Christmas. Let it grow up with her, develop into a fiercely protective guard dog. Chew the arm off anyone who ever got within three feet of her again.

He scrubbed his face as if that would rub away the protective—and quite frankly, Neanderthal—reactions he had around Maribelle. This parenting thing? He wondered how anyone survived it.

He found a few more pictures with Adelaide included where she clearly was taking a selfie. She had quite the smile. She certainly used it enough. It wasn't practiced, though, not like so many women he'd met over the years: hardened New York women who could sum up a man in under thirty seconds.

Adelaide's looseness was new to him. That's what it was.

She was freewheeling, easy-going, yet would punch a fish if needed. That last thought made him chuckle—and he was glad for her protective nature. He hoped like hell she'd not ever have to exercise it to the extent he'd had to.

7

———

Addy and Scarlett stood in Maribelle's closet. Scarlett ran her hand over the hangers holding all of Maribelle's little dresses.

Scarlett slowly shook her head. "You were right. Not a single pair of leggings." She tsked. "I am so disappointed in that man."

Something told Addy The Exalted One wouldn't mind Scarlett's disappointment. Maribelle getting dirty? Now that would call for some serious displeasure. Or the fact that Addy sort of broke the 'no stranger' rule. But Scarlett was family, not a stranger.

"Tragic, right?" Addy glanced back at Maribelle, who was preoccupied with folding the twenty-seven pairs of leggings and little T-shirts Scarlett had brought from Giraffe and Jammies. "Thanks for bringing them. You're a lifesaver."

Her sister was more than that to her. Her sister was everything. Her best friend and confidant—if the woman remembered to actually *tell* her things.

"I might forgive you now for holding out on the news of," Adelaide lowered her voice, "you know who."

Her sister's mind was a sieve. Information in, information out in seconds.

Scarlett arched an eyebrow. "You mean your super-hot boss? The guy whose picture you swooned over for years?"

"I didn't *swoon*. I had one encounter fourteen years ago which he clearly doesn't remember, and I don't, really."

'Uh-huh." Scarlett moved closer to her. "Let's have the details. For my book. Like what's he like?" Scarlett whispered. "Is he as gorgeous as his pictures? What does he smell like?"

"No." Addy would not give Scarlett any fodder for her Great American Erotica Novel she wrote at night. Even if Addy did have a super-erotic dream about him last night. She hadn't had one of those about him in over a decade. Back then, it was all about him drawing her close, kissing her until she was slithering down the side of a wall. Her dreams involving him always had her against a wall.

But now? Let's say she'd graduated to the big leagues on salacious possibilities. Slamming her against shower tiles, pitching her forward over the baseboard of a bed, and thrusting into her until the headboard was banging against the wall.

It had to be all his rule-setting and stern voice and child protectiveness. Drop her to her knees now…

Scarlett eyed her. "At least give me his thirst trap number." Her sister was always rating guys on a scale of one to ten based on their "pure animal magnetism," as she put it.

"No way." But honestly? One hundred.

Addy moved back into the room where Maribelle was pulling on a pair of leggings—or trying to. Addy moved to help her. The little girl had chosen yellow, of course.

"Nice pick, Queen Maribelle."

As soon as they got her outfitted in a pair of leggings and matching top with yellow and blue butterflies decorated in sequins, Maribelle danced up and down. She moved her legs around. "I like these. I can't wait to show Daddy. Take a picture and text it to him."

Scarlett wagged her eyebrows. "You have his phone number?"

"To provide updates." Though it did feel a little thrilling to have *the* Ashton Scott's phone number.

Maribelle cocked a pose worthy of a supermodel and Addy captured it on her phone.

"Send it, send it." Maribelle danced up and down.

"Doing it now."

Maribelle then began to run around the room, having a sudden case of the zoomies.

Addie's phone buzzed with a return text from Ash.

<<What is my child wearing>>

The Exalted One was a little miffed?

<<Her new play clothes. You did say to get whatever she needed.>>

Three dots blinked at her under her message back to him. They went on forever.

Scarlett peered over her shoulder. "He's waffling. Why?"

Addy jerked her hand back. "Hey. This is confidential." She glanced over at Maribelle, who was completely preoccupied, enjoying her clothing freedom by dancing around the room.

Scarlett rolled her eyes.

.   .   .

<<Here another 36 hours. Will call M later.>>

So, New York had its fists around him.

<<<Storytime is at 7:15 if you can make it.>>

<<Dinner meeting. Will attempt.>>

"Attempt?" Scarlett guffawed.

"Hey, cut it out." She pulled her phone back to her chest to shield the screen. Sure, a normal human being would say "try," but she'd give him a break. She took another peek when the phone pinged again.

<<Thank you for getting her favorite color.>>

That was a message she did show Scarlett. "See? He knows her favorite color. He definitely loves her."

"Well, give him the parent of the year award."

"Shhh." She glanced at Maribelle, who was paying no attention to them. She was reorganizing her dolls, telling them about the fashion show they'd get later of all her new outfits.

Scarlett leaned closer to Addy. "Still, I can't believe he's not taken. Rich, hot, single parent. It's ideal. You should so go for it, Addy."

"Oh, come on." She pulled a knee up higher on the bed and faced her sister. "But word is definitely out. You'll never guess who showed up here the other night. Sally Albrecchio."

"Shut up. She hasn't blown out of this town? I knew she was full of bluster. All that, 'I'm going to be an actress,' crap."

"She almost ruined Ash's suit with her drool."

Scarlett gasped. "She got that close? Of course, she did."

"I'm shocked she didn't conveniently trip into his crotch."

Scarlett's face shifted. "I am so putting that scene in my book. Do it to him. Then tell me all the details. Make sure your hand lands—"

"I am not." As if she'd dare to have her hand *land*. Still, her blood started to ricochet every which way in her veins thinking about said landing. Her face getting close enough to inhale his shaving cream and linen scent? Her hands landing on his chest? Or other places? She squeezed her thighs together a little at the mere thought. It was one thing to have nighttime dreams, another to start daydreaming about him. To be honest, her attraction to him made no sense whatsoever. He wasn't exactly the most inviting man. Perhaps she was a masochist in the making.

Scarlett frowned. "How did Sally get invited here anyway?"

"She's on the board of the Moorsville Girls Academy." Adelaide glanced at Maribelle, who was now organizing her dolls by height. "Maribelle's going there soon."

Scarlett tsked. "Man, this girl's life is truly tragic, isn't it? Losing your mother and then going to a boarding school? We have to accelerate things here…"

Scarlett's face adopted The Look—the one that made Addy's spine freeze. Ash thought Addy would require rules? Boundaries were shifting sand to her sister. "We?"

"Like I'm going to let another female in this town, even one six years old, face a lifetime of boredom? Being trained to be another Sally? You know my purpose in life. Yours, too."

Shaking things up *had* been the Bloom sisters' specialty. "I can't. I agreed to some… guidelines."

Scarlett's eyebrows shot up. "You? Seriously?"

"I can follow rules."

"Uh-huh."

Maribelle ran up to them and held up a pink pair of leggings. "I want to wear these tomorrow."

Scarlett brightened. "Hey, I have an idea. Let's go outside and try to find that old tree house in the back. You like to climb trees?"

Maribelle shrugged. "I dunno."

"Or…" Scarlett slowly swung her gaze to Addy. "We could introduce Maribelle to the horses."

Maribelle gasped. "You have a horse?"

Addy shook her head. "Sorry, Queen Maribelle, we're not allowed to leave."

She scowled. "But whyyyy?"

"Are you sure he's not a sadist?" Scarlett at least whispered that theory. She then leaned back and raised her voice. "He's out of town. He'll never know."

Maribelle ran over and gave Scarlett's legs a big hug. "I'd love to see your horse."

Her sister—who was the worst influence ever—smiled down at her. "His name is Beano. He farts. A lot."

Maribelle slapped her hand over her mouth and giggled. "You said fart."

Scarlett pulled her up onto her lap and the two of them stared at Addy.

Ganged up on. "Okay, but only if Stevens says it's okay." That wouldn't be breaking any of Ash's rules.

"Yay! You're the best nanny ever." Maribelle clapped her

hands and bounced on Scarlett. "I'll go find her." She slipped down and landed on her feet.

Addy groaned. "Thanks a lot, Scarlett."

"What? Fresh air would do that child, who is entirely too happy to have leggings and T-shirts, some good. And what is all this Stevens crap? Is that seriously her name?"

"Don't know. I follow Ash's lead. Do what he says."

"Ooo, so k-i-n-k-y."

Maribelle spun and stared at her. "What's kinky?"

Scarlett's mouth dropped open. "She can spell."

Addy ignored her. "It's what happens when your hair gets a dent in it from a ponytail holder. And Maribelle, let's…"

The little girl was out the door like a shot.

Addy rose and turned to her sister. "I can't get fired."

Scarlett joined her and hooked her arm into Addy's. "No, you can't. You need to trip into Ashton Scott's glorious crotch before Sally does. Then, report in. I want measurements."

Addy didn't need to trip into him to know. If her dream last night was any indication, Ash Scott was indeed a very big fish.

8

———————

Ash stared at the picture on his phone screen and nearly ran over a woman on the sidewalk. "Pardon me."

He side-stepped, allowing her to pass. His gaze jerked back to the scene on his phone. His daughter sat atop a horse six times her size. A strange woman with a mass of blond curly hair held the bridle.

He pinched the screen wider. Dots of mud colored Maribelle's legs and T-shirt. A huge smile brightened her face. It was the only good thing about the scene.

He dialed. Loosened his tie. Swallowed once, twice to punch down the knot in his throat.

"Hi, Mr. Scott."

Jesus, even her voice smiled. "There are no horses living on my property." He raised his hand to hail a cab. He didn't have the patience to wait for a car service to retrieve him.

"Oh, good, you got the picture. Maribelle made me send it right away because—"

"Miss Bloom. Do you remember my very simple rules? No leaving the premises. No strangers." There could have been half a dozen photographers sneaking behind bushes.

God knew he'd watched them capture his every move outside while in New York. "I've been calling for thirty minutes."

A yellow cab cut across two lanes of traffic and screeched to a halt in front of him.

"Stevens said it was okay. To leave, I mean," she said quickly. "You never answered my earlier text and then I put my phone on silent to not scare the horses."

He had ignored all of his text messages lately, too, hadn't he? Mostly to get away from O'Connor buzzing him every few minutes. And old girlfriends noticing he was back in town. Who was he kidding? His one-night stands.

He yanked open the door, folded himself inside. "Where are you?"

"My family's farm."

"37 Broadway," he said to the cab driver.

"No, 12 State Road."

His whole face tensed. "Not you. But what was that address?" The cab lurched into traffic, nearly toppling him over.

She repeated it, and he quickly mapped it. Ten miles from where she and his daughter should be. He knew that old place. They gave Saturday morning horseback riding lessons —if one could call getting on an eighteen-year-old horse to ride around a ring in circles for an hour a "lesson."

He brought the phone back to his ear. "Miss Bloom." No answer. The phone was dead. "Goddammit." He dialed again, and she answered.

"Let me put Maribelle on."

"No, Adelaide. Adelaide?" The rustle of fabric sounded. He was going to punch a hole in the taxi ceiling out of frustration.

"Daddy! Daddy! I rode a horse. His name is Beano because he farts. Isn't that funny?"

His gut lurched at hearing her voice. "Very funny. Are you okay? The horse didn't scare you?" He had to clutch the tattered headrest in front of him to keep from bouncing all over the back seat. "Easy there," he said to the driver —as if that would have any effect. Just like his words did little to impact the new nanny he'd unwisely hired.

"At first, but then Addy was on one side and Scarlett was on the other and they kept a hold of him the whole time even though I asked him to let us run."

"We need to walk before we run, my little Belle."

"Yeah." A light sigh sounded. "That's what Addy said."

Score one for the nanny. It still didn't get her out of the negative point zone.

"Daddy, when are you coming home? I need to show you my new legs."

He chuckled. "New legs, huh?" They were probably filthy dirty from what he could tell in the photo.

Adelaide's voice rang out in the background. The lightness of her tone irritated him to no end.

"Leg-gings," Maribelle corrected.

A little laugh came out of his throat from that one. "I'll be home tomorrow, my Belle. Please, put Adelaide back on."

"Addy, Addy, Daddy wants you." A loud giggle sounded. "That rhymed."

When was the last time his little girl smiled so much? Laughed so much? It was strange, this hollow feeling that grew in his chest whenever he was away from her, too. Like a piece of him was missing.

"Okay, here she is. But don't talk with your mad face, Daddy, okay?"

More damned shuffling sounded in his ear.

"Am I fired?" Adelaide at least sounded contrite, though the usual, internal sunshine poured from her voice.

"That depends. Are you at my house?"

An annoying scoff left her throat. "No, dang it. In the barn. We have three more horses to pet."

Another unwanted laugh tried to form in his throat. He choked it back. He was being played, wasn't he? She had a way of making his rightful anger drop too easily, start bending his resolve to keep some order when it came to his daughter.

"Mr. Scott, would it count if technically this whole situation wasn't my fault?"

"I've heard that before." Had he ever. "Then whose fault would it be?"

"It was my sister Scarlett's idea. Nobody could ever say no to her."

Ah, the other woman in the photograph. "I could."

"I'll bet you could. So, like, how fired am I? Mad-pretend fired? Or like for-real fired?"

She'd gone through this before, hadn't she?

Truth was, he would love to not need this woman. Staring again at his phone, his daughter's happy face, smeared with dirt and a leaf in her hair, smiled up at him. Maribelle liked her, and she hadn't been happy in so long. "You're not fired."

"Oh, good. Because I'd miss Maribelle. And I did this for her. At the Moorsville Girl's Academy, they do a lot of outdoors stuff, including horseback riding. They even come to our farm for the younger kids. Our horses are tame, and they get used to being on an animal twenty times their size. Maribelle will now be ahead of her class."

"I see." He should have thought of that himself. Moorsville did pride itself on giving women esteem not only through academics but sports as well.

"Consider it a personalized learning pathway. Like the book and—"

"Alright. Alright." This woman could justify a jewelry heist, couldn't she?

"And being outside is good for kids. Helps them get their ya-ya's out."

She also couldn't stop explaining herself. "Of course, but—"

"If you'd ever like to bring Maribelle out here yourself, ride with her, you can. I guess I didn't think you'd want to be the first one to show her a horse. She'd got a good seat on her."

"Naturally—"

"Given all the polo trophies you won, I'd have guessed she'd already been riding before but she said—"

"Adelaide." This woman also could not keep her lips closed. "Don't leave again without my explicit permission, understand?" He'd have to find out what Stevens was thinking, letting his daughter run off to a farm where any number of things could have happened.

"Yes, sir."

Finally, she spoke two words that made sense to him. "I have to stay another night, but I'll be home on Thursday. Maribelle and I have a photoshoot in the afternoon." Damned PR thing again. "In a dress, please."

"Whatever you'd like."

"I'd like to not have to worry about my daughter." The truth rang clear in his mind with his words. He cleared the growing frog in his throat.

An audible swallow sounded. "I promise I won't ever let anything happen to her. I mean, I promise-promise."

He felt oddly assured by that. She may be infuriating, but she did seem to care about his daughter. "Of course. And… thank you."

The cab lurched in front of the building where he'd been summoned for yet another bullshit meeting with Saunders. "Just… pick up the phone when I call. And try not to have her roll around in the mud, please?"

"How did you know that was next on the agenda?" She laughed. "Kidding."

"How did you know about my horseback riding days anyway?"

"Google. How did anyone find anything before it?"

There was some truth to that. "I've often wondered the same. We'll talk later, Adelaide."

When he hung up, images of the stables of the Emerson Boarding School where he spent most of his youth flashed in his mind. It'd been a fairly simple life albeit privileged. He knew it then. He knew it now.

He often wondered what it would have been like had he gone to public school in Moorsville. He sure as hell wouldn't have won any polo matches there, not that his history of being an ace Number Two player did him any good today. Still, a jolt of energy returned to his limbs at remembering his days on the field. He loved scaring the hell out of the opposing team's best player in his same position.

So, Adelaide knew about all that, probably having seen his trophies in his rarely-used childhood bedroom at home. And she'd Googled him. He guessed that was to be expected. His ego, however, did something it should not have done: it liked that she was interested.

Scarlett popped her gum. "You are blushing like a virgin on prom night."

"Am not." Addy toed a small twig on the barn floor.

Maribelle tugged on her hand. "Why are you so red, Addy?"

Scarlett cocked her hip and pursed her lips. "She likes a boy."

Maribelle pursed her lips like she'd sucked on a lemon. "Boys are icky."

Scarlett crouched down to her level. "Why don't you go pet Miss Carmichael-Peabody over there?" She pointed at the pony munching from a straw bale at the end of the barn. Maribelle broke off into a run.

"Walk," Addy called. "You don't want to scare the pony."

Maribelle slowed and stepped gingerly up to the old beast.

Scarlett huffed. "That pony wouldn't budge if a bomb went off next to her. Now…" She turned to Addy. "Spill it. You still have the hots for him."

"Who?"

"Oh, don't give me that. I know you better than anyone." Scarlett hooked her arm and led her a few further feet away from Maribelle. The little girl stroked the pony's neck and cooed, totally oblivious to the interrogation Addy was about to endure.

Her sister looked her straight in the eye. "You got all loose-tongued when you were fourteen and did now with him again."

Scarlett was the only person she'd ever told about "the run-in" with Ashton Scott. The day she'd realized she lived in one world and he an entirely different one.

"No. He doesn't affect me the same way *at all*. I've moved on." Liar, liar, nanny on fire. But what could she do? Admit to the fact a dam of pent-up imaginings around the man broke? Voice aloud that she kept dreaming of him doing things to her—wickedly sinful things? It'd be too humiliating, especially since he'd so thoroughly dismissed her years ago.

Scarlett gentled her voice. "You're doing that thing again, aren't you? He totally snubbed you and you took him off the menu forever. You glossed over the negative experience like you always do."

"He was never on the menu."

"Menus change." She crossed her arms. "You're grown-ass adults now. Your palates have matured."

"I *work* for him."

"Not illegal. Let's face it, you haven't been out with a guy since—"

"Don't say his name!" Her sister wouldn't.

"Bryson. There, I said it. Or Fuckface, if you prefer."

Addy stomped off towards Maribelle but was stopped by Scarlett's voice behind her.

"You let Sally get to you again, didn't you?"

Lightning flashed through Addy's blood. She spun on her sister. "No. I didn't. I… can't go there."

A sweet black mare stuck her head out of the stall nearest her. Addy ran her fingers down her soft nose. It was calming in a way, brought her back to the present instead of lurching her back to the horrible weeks following the breakup with Bryson that Sally couldn't stop rubbing in her face again and again. It was the woman's favorite thing to do—find cracks in people's armor and then widen it so the arrows could get inside.

Scarlett scooted closer to her. "Go there? You most definitely should. What better way to get revenge on Sally for what she did to you and Bryson than taking away her prospects? Or she will land him and then—"

"He's smarter than that. He would never fall for her." Her chin lifted so sharply, the mare's head danced between the bars. Addy cooed a little at her. "He would never ever end up with a woman like Sally Albrecchio."

The mere thought of Ash with a woman like Sally? It'd be like Mr. Darcy ending up with the loud-mouthed Lydia instead of the magnificent Elizabeth Bennett.

"He won't if you finally admit you're kind of perfect for him."

"What are you talking about?"

"He needs someone to balance him. I could tell from that text exchange. Remember. We *know* things. It's our superpower."

"I don't think he'd see it that way." She put her forehead against the horse's. "Besides, it's not exactly up to just me."

When she turned back to her sister, Scarlett had her arms crossed and eyebrows practically to the barn roof. "So, you *have* thought about it. Well, you're in luck. He hasn't dated a woman in over a year. His…" She glanced over at Maribelle, who was wholly occupied with whispering to the pony, probably giving it fashion advice, like what color horse blanket would look best on her. "…cock has to be ready to explode."

She doubted that, but… "You looked him up?"

"Of course." She widened her eyes. "Didn't you?"

"Yes, but then… I stopped. It felt weird."

"Or it made you jealous."

Her sister knew too much about her. Her summation of the situation was dead-on and it made her feel awful. "All I found were pictures of him with women."

Scarlett nodded once, sharply. "Yep. Jelly."

Now it was her turn to roll her eyes. The truth was it did bother her to see him with all those women. And not airheads, either. He went out with newscasters and fellow attorneys, and there was even a female judge he'd once dated. His varied history was impressive. And it reminded her what he'd told her all those years ago. She wasn't in his—or their—league.

She leaned against the barn door. "Do you know why they had to leave New York?" Her curiosity still couldn't be tamed. She hadn't had time to dig very deep for any real information on him, and what she did find didn't go beyond the fact Maribelle's mother had died and Ash turned out to be her father. "You hear everything down at Peppermint Sweet. So?"

Scarlet flapped her arms for Addy to move even closer. "Well, the dish is as soon as Maribelle's fortune was revealed—"

"Fortune?"

"The kid is loaded. Kate apparently was an entrepreneur. Makeup line. Clothing label. And now, Maribelle will never have to work ever in her life. We're talking buy-your-own-Caribbean-island wealth."

"But why come here then?" It made no sense. The man could have gone anywhere.

"Apparently, all these women have come forward with various stories. Affairs so they can get press. And even two wanting DNA tests for their own kid. All probably trying to get Maribelle's fortune. You'll see there isn't a single picture of him on a date since that day. People were hounding him to no end, and Maribelle, too."

Addy's gaze moved to Maribelle. "Hounding her? How?"

Her sister leaned over so her face came into view. "I recognize that look. You did it again, didn't you? You have the hots for your boss, *and* you have fallen in love with his little girl."

"I do not have the hots for him," she hissed. Okay, maybe she did a little, but Scarlett would push her to the nth degree if she admitted it. "Besides, all of this talk is moot. He would never be interested in someone like me. He's Ashton Scott."

"Adelaide Bloom, I don't ever want to hear you say that again. It wouldn't hurt to get to know him. You never know."

Oh, she knew alright. Adelaide Bloom had a past that would never fit with Ash. If only she could keep it from him. She'd worked hard to have everyone in Moorsville forget. *Ha.* As if they ever would. It was only a matter of time before Ash learned of it—probably from Sally herself.

Maribelle skipped up to them. "The pony wants a carrot. She told me."

"She did, huh?"

One thing Addy knew for sure: she needed to make sure she stuck around past the probation period. She and Maribelle got along well, and she'd punch more than a fish if anyone got near her.

As for Ash? She now understood the tension running under his skin like the Amazon River. She really needed to get better at online sleuthing.

9

———

Ash took his front steps two at a time. He'd figure out how to get the rental car back to the airport later.

"She insists on a DNA test," O'Connor said through the phone line.

He tugged a hand through his hair. He might be bald after this phone call. "I never touched that woman. How would a conception even be possible?"

"Perception is everything." O'Connor sounded too calm after delivering this news. "But it was good you got out of New York when you did."

Ash stepped through the front door and met total silence. Where the devil was everyone? Then again, he'd jetted home a few hours early and had only texted Stevens. New York got on his nerves, not to mention they were getting nowhere on the Transom case in person.

He headed to his office. "Do something. A statement. Counter gossip leaked to social. Anything." The fact that he needed a public relations rep at all galled him to no end, so he'd like to see some action.

Ash switched the phone to his other ear as he dropped his bag in the club chair in front of his desk.

"Laying low is doing something. Anna just wants her fifteen minutes of fame. Going with all barrels loaded will look like you have something to hide. Listen, I'm flying down in a few hours. If you'd waited, we could have flown in together."

"Needed to get back." He needed to see his little girl, and waiting for O'Connor to get from his office on the other side of town to LaGuardia would have taken too long.

"We'll do this photoshoot today and use the father-daughter photos to counter, okay?"

He grunted a reply, then angrily hit "end call." More talk would be useless. And new photos of him and Maribelle playing the happy family? They wouldn't counter a whisper.

Sunshine cutting in from the window facing the backyard landed on his chest. It beckoned him closer. Outside, Maribelle was running across the yard, her hair flying in all directions, so oblivious to the cruelties of the world—like people only wanting you for money, or status, or ridiculous "likes" and "follows."

He turned away. A loud splat against the windowpane caused him to spin back to the glass. A long trail of water ran down the side. What the hell?

A distant, happy shriek finally drifted through the air, and his mouth lifted into a smile. An automatic reaction at hearing his daughter. She was like sunshine on his soul. Everything about her lightened the air around him.

He followed Maribelle's happy squeals through his office door and down the side hall, through the kitchen to the back terrace. He stepped through the door and a large jelly-like ball landed square on his chest. It burst, dousing him with water. What the ever-loving…?

A water balloon. Someone had thrown a fucking water balloon at him.

"Oh, crap." Adelaide's voice rang in the air—hell, down his spine. "You're home early."

Maribelle's giggle followed. "That's two points! And you're 'it,' Daddy!"

He held out the lapels of his jacket and shook off water drops. "What… are you doing?"

"Addy got you, so now you have to chase us."

"Oh?" He arched an eyebrow in the nanny's direction. "I just got in, and we have a photoshoot in two hours. We need to get her cleaned up."

"Water's clean." Adelaide stepped closer and lifted a pink, quivering water balloon in one hand, a blue one in the other. "She's not getting dirty."

And there went her smile. Anyone with a smile like that would use it often. She smoothed things over with her wide grin, made lesser men weak in the knees. Why was this woman still in this town anyway? She seemed smart enough, and certainly pretty enough, to have whatever she wanted.

Maribelle huffed. "You're going back to work, aren't you?" Her little pout was most definitely fierce. "Don't go back to work, Daddy. I have to show you the tree house we found outside."

"I have to, princess."

"Queen."

He gave Addy a look that he hoped conveyed his thoughts: you're responsible for this.

Adelaide tossed one of the water balloons a few inches in the air and caught it. "Maybe he thinks he's outnumbered."

He was definitely that.

"Or…" She pursed her lips. "He can't catch us."

Maribelle gasped and quickly ran out the back. "You can't catch me, Daddy."

Ash's gaze locked onto Adelaide. "Manipulating me?"

"I wouldn't dare. Got anyone you'd like to nail, proverbially? I mean, other than me. Oh, that came out wrong. I mean, wanna join us? There's a bucket by your feet with at least twenty more. See if you can get us."

He glanced down. Sure enough, there was a bucket full of brightly colored balloons stretched wide with water. "It would be highly inappropriate. I'm certainly not going to hit someone who works for me with a water balloon."

"If I was sixteen, maybe. But I consent if you need it. It's harmless fun." Her lips inched up again. "Unless you think your aim isn't good."

He picked one up out of the bucket, leaned back, and shot it across the yard to land on a huge oak tree. It burst on impact, sending a satisfying cascade of water in all directions. It felt great to, as she put it, 'nail something.' Damned great.

A soft slap hit his leg. Maribelle had thrown a balloon at him. It didn't break, and she giggled.

He shrugged off his jacket and laid it over a garden chair. "Well, since I'm 'it.'" He picked up Maribelle's balloon.

Adelaide jiggled the pink balloon in her hand. "She's fast."

"Oh, but I'm sure I can land one on you."

"Many men have tried to catch me." She leaned back, and within seconds, he was doused with yet another water balloon.

Alright, then. He wasn't interested in *catching* her. But landing a harmless water balloon across her ass? Most definitely on today's docket.

She was game and a full-grown adult who consented to be doused with every single water balloon from this bucket if he had anything to do with it. Maybe he'd leave one or two for her. He was nothing if not fair.

He dropped Maribelle's balloon into the bucket and

rolled up his shirt sleeves. He then reached down to get the largest one he could find. When he glanced up both Maribelle and Adelaide were nowhere to be seen.

"Here's the deal," he called out into the yard. "I land this water balloon on our esteemed nanny, and she not only ensures an on-time departure this afternoon but also doesn't speak a word during our photoshoot."

"It's not healthy to keep things inside." Adelaide's voice came from behind one of the large black walnut trees in the center of the yard.

"Not everything needs to be discussed. Don't think you can be silent?"

"What do I get if I land another one on you?"

Maribelle's little laugh sounded in the air. She was hiding behind the other tree standing a few feet from where Adelaide hid. "Daddy builds my tree castle."

Her negotiation point was flawed, but he appreciated her effort. "A tree castle, huh?"

"Well, that tree house has seen better days," Adelaide said, "and a queen needs her castle."

Magic, castles… This woman was planting some ideas in his daughter's head. Still, he'd loved that tree house as a boy. He'd spent a lot of summers tucked away up there.

"So, is it a deal?"

"Deal. If you can," she added defiantly.

Oh, he could alright. He strode toward them.

In the end, it turned out Adelaide Bloom had a pair of long legs. She was able to dart and weave and avoid his first attempt at landing a water balloon on her. He was in decent shape, so his wind stayed with him and he didn't crack a sweat. He shouldn't have been out acting like a twelve-year-old, but still, it felt damned good to be doing something other than sitting in a conference room or a taxi cab.

"I thought you were a runner?" Adelaide asked when he missed her twice.

"That means I can last longer than you." He jogged back up to the terrace and got two more. She stood in the middle of the yard, taunting him. Her dark hair lifted in the breeze, and her eyes sparkled with bravado.

The idea of this woman's lips being closed was too good of a deal to miss. He needed some peace and quiet today, so he wasn't about to let her win this one.

He raised his arm, and she darted to the left. He at least had the wherewithal to not let loose his balloon weapon on his target yet.

Maribelle danced up and down on the side at the spectacle. "You can do it, Daddy."

He smiled at her and—smack! Adelaide had landed a water balloon right where the first one had—his chest. He looked down at his soaking wet shirt and then back up at her.

She shrugged. "I was on the softball team."

Oh, really? He retrieved two more balloons. All he needed was to land one balloon, and he'd be damned if he didn't make it happen.

He spun to face one smug-looking nanny and his gleeful little girl. He hadn't been around this much female energy in a while. Adelaide certainly had some vitality, her eyes clear and bright and her signature smile firmly in place.

He fingered the two balloons. They felt good in his hands.

The chase continued to the corner of the house. He then darted to the left when Adelaide threw a balloon at him with all her might. She definitely had an arm on her. Leg muscles, too.

He finally managed to get one square between her shoulder blades when she tried to fake him out. It burst in the center and a cascade of water flowed down her back, wetting her T-shirt to the bone.

"And he scores," she laughed. "I knew you had it in you."

He straightened, finally feeling a tad winded. "Because you know things?"

She tilted her head. "I suspected you needed that win. Not," she pointed her finger at him, "that I would ever let you win."

"Oh, I could win, alright, if we had more balloons. I was biding my time."

She laughed. "Okay, three out of five next time."

Maribelle ran up to him and wrapped her arms around his legs. "Addy is good, isn't she, Daddy?"

He slapped his hand across his very wet chest and nodded his chin toward Adelaide. "I'm honored. You are a worthy opponent."

The heaviness of his trip that had sat on his shoulders like a yoke had released. He was beginning to see what Maribelle saw in her. Adelaide Bloom was maddening—all the questioning and justifications and general wordiness—but a sparkle showed through her that cleared the air. Nothing was too significant, nothing too hard around her.

He was noticing too much. He turned away and stretched his neck. A face stared at him from the azaleas, a cell phone held up. Fuck, they were being filmed.

"Hey, you. Who are you?" Maribelle released her hold, and he strode with some force toward the guy, who stumbled backward. By the time he'd reached the bushes on the far side of the yard, the man was gone.

"Damn it to hell." His hand returned to tug at his hair.

Adelaide's panting was behind him. "Who was that?"

"A photographer." He waved his hand over her. "And you looking like a walking wet T-shirt contest. Inside, everyone. *Now.*"

Maribelle ran up behind Addy and clutched at her legs. Her bottom lip quivered.

"Get her upstairs and ready for the photoshoot. I have to make a phone call." He couldn't wait for O'Connor to get here. He needed a warning right now because that video? It was landing on social as he stood there.

Maribelle burst into tears as soon as Addy picked her up. "Mama never yelled."

Kill him now. "I'm sorry I yelled, Maribelle," he said to her. "I'll be upstairs soon. You can show me your… hair ribbon."

The nanny's eyes were round as saucers. "Good plan." Her voice was hard—full of steel. "So important right now."

The nanny had a spine. It wasn't welcomed at the moment. She had no idea how pictures of him running around acting like an idiot would set him back.

"Mr. Scott?" Stevens appeared on the terrace. "Chief O'Connor just pulled up. Shall I show him to your office?" Her gaze ran up and down the three of them standing there, wet and pissed off.

"Do that. Thanks." He turned back to Adelaide and Maribelle. "I'll be up soon. We leave in an hour."

Adelaide turned without a word and took a sniffling Maribelle up the stone steps. Ash joined Stevens on the terrace.

"Need a towel?"

He straightened his shirt. "No."

"Mr. Scott, I realize this isn't my business—"

"Then don't say it."

She sighed. "Is it wise for you to be flirting with Miss Bloom? I mean, I know everyone is an adult but… *that nanny?*" She arched an eyebrow.

A familiar feeling rode up his spine. Stevens thought something was going on between him and Adelaide? Hardly.

"She's a grown adult." Why did every person on this planet believe he was such a horndog? *Oh, maybe because he'd dated a hundred women,* his conscience barked.

Stevens nodded a few times. "I get it. You like her, but I've heard some things—"

His hand sliced the air. No more getting information third-hand from anyone. He was fucking sick of people telling him who other people were. "Maribelle likes her. That's enough."

He himself, however, could not afford to like her beyond being good for his daughter. If he had to live like a monk for the rest of his days to ensure Maribelle's reputation wasn't soiled by his, so be it.

10

———

Hot lights spotlighted Ash and Maribelle. He shifted in the chair and heaved a sigh.

"Here, Daddy, you need some, too." Maribelle rolled the lavender stick on his arm. Addy didn't have the heart to tell her the oil wouldn't work. The man needed to soak in a vat of it for an effect to take hold. He'd been huffing and puffing his way through this whole photoshoot.

Maribelle wasn't doing much better. She refused to smile and kept squirming on her father's lap. Who could blame her? Once someone had the freedom of stretch leggings, having to go back to a dress was torture.

She gave the girl credit, though. Maribelle picked the "least scratchy" of the bunch for the photoshoot. It was a white dress made of Swiss dot with little daisies all over it.

The fact that the girl knew it was Swiss dot fabric was amazing. As Addy had calmed her down from her earlier crying spell and got Maribelle and herself dressed, she'd learned a lot about clothes.

Once Addy showed a smidge of interest, Maribelle became a walking Project Runway. Addy now had a near-master's level degree in fabrics thanks to Maribelle showing off various samples from her closet.

Suede can't get wet.

Acrylic has excellent color retention.

The highest quality cotton comes from Egypt.

Apparently, Maribelle had spent most of her time with her mother in a closet. But then again, *supermodel.*

The camera clicking sped up, the lights behind the big umbrellas glowed, and Ash stretched his neck to the side. While he looked amazing in that dark blue suit that brought out the sparkle in his eyes, a zoo animal showed more enthusiasm. On the plus side, he looked like he was about to storm someone's castle.

Yeah, she'd moved on from smutty shower dreams to smutty pirate dreams about him.

Chief O'Connor stuffed his hands in his trousers. "Let's lose the tie."

Adelaide nodded vigorously. She lowered her voice so only Chief could hear. "And the coat. Roll up his sleeves." Even if he rocked a suit like nobody's business, it was too formal, proper, detached for a father-daughter picture. She glanced out the window. "Better still, what do you say to taking this outside?" She pointed across the street at Brickman Park.

Ash sliced his blue eyes her way, and a little tingle formed along her spine. He really did have such beautiful eyes, blue and glittery. It was a shame they sat in a face so grumpy.

O'Connor wrinkled his eyebrows. "Great idea, nanny girl." He lifted his chin toward Ash, who was making a valiant attempt at balancing Maribelle on his knee. "Let's take this to the park. Make it more real. Maybe in front of that tree over there."

Addy squeezed her hands together at her breastbone. "It's an historic tree, too."

O'Connor snapped his fingers. "Done."

Ash's right eyebrow arched up like Mr. Spock's. "*New York Magazine* wants to see tree bark in the shot?"

"New York wants to see you being a father."

"I am a father." His roar made Addy—and Maribelle— jump. Ash tightened his arm around her to keep her from falling off. "Sorry, Maribelle." He pressed a kiss into her hair.

Chief threw up his hands. "Of course, Ash. It's just…" His eyes sliced to the side at Addy. "We can discuss it later." He strode to the door and opened it. "Trust me on this one? Jenkins, do you mind?"

The photographer hitched his photography bag onto his shoulder. "Your dime."

Ash eased Maribelle off his lap. "You know what happened the last time you said, 'Trust me,' O'Connor."

He slapped his hand over his chest. "Horrors, the headlines stopped."

The fact this man could talk to Ash Scott that way spoke volumes. They were friends. Ash smirked at him. His bark was worse than his bite. Though in that suit? The thought of him biting was tantalizing.

Maribelle squirmed in her dress. "I'm sooo itchy." Her little body wilted like a noodle against her father's leg.

Adelaide grabbed her hands and spun her in a circle. "It'll be over before you know it. And mine does, too, a little." She figured wearing a dress in solidarity was one way to get Maribelle back into a dress as "directed by the public relations department," according to Stevens.

Addy was getting Stevens some lavender oil soon, too. The woman could use it.

As they made their way to the door that led to the stairs leading down to the street, Ash stuffed his hands into his pockets. He cleared his throat. "Adelaide. Got a second?"

She nodded. "Maribelle, mind helping Chief down the stairs?"

The little girl beamed over at her and took the man's hand. His eyes grew wide but quickly got with the program. "Why, thank you, Miss Scott."

Maribelle skipped out with Chief, and Ash gestured for Addy to follow suit. His gaze ran up and down her. He then lowered his voice. "Thank you." So grumbly.

"For?"

"Helping make Maribelle more comfortable. The…" He waved his hand over her. "… dress. The whole female unity thing." He stuck a finger in his collar, looking as if his skin itched, too.

She gave off a half-laugh. "Why, this old thing?" She sent her fingertips to her breastbone. Jesus, she'd adopted some weird Scarlett O'Hara thing for a second. It was his suit. It made her brain fritz. It didn't help he was always in one, too.

They took the stairs down slowly, his steps rigid. Her skirt fanned out a little in the air, and her hands pushed the fabric down instinctively.

Chief and Maribelle were waiting for them outside the glass door. He was telling her something, making her laugh.

"You trust him. Chief O'Connor, I mean." He must have if he let Maribelle walk out with her.

"I do. Listen." He paused. "O'Connor tells me the photographer this afternoon? He caught you on camera. It might show up on Facebook or something."

She waved one hand. "Not a fan of social media. And that photographer? I recognized him. He's a local guy, harmless. He wanted to capture The Exalted One."

"Ah, you saw the article." He shook his head, took more steps down. He paused on the steps. "No photographer is harmless. I won't have Maribelle treated like a zoo animal."

"But like a princess locked away in a castle who can't get

dirty?" She injected a lilt into her voice, trying to make the question more palpable.

"Do you always talk to your bosses like this?"

She swallowed. "Sorry."

She wasn't really, and she was still miffed at him for being so crotchety over a simple water balloon fight, but she had to let it go. He had to stop worrying about this afternoon, too. The man had spent too much time in New York where everyone seemed perpetually on edge.

"Listen, the guy who took the pictures was Hamish MacLean. He still lives in his mother's basement. He'll probably load them onto his blog that has two people who read it —himself and his mother."

He at least chuckled at that. "Let's hope."

"And sorry about… earlier. The water balloon, I mean. I wasn't trying to get out of line. It was just fun."

One side of his mouth inched up. "It was, to be honest." He continued to walk down.

She laughed. "Well, thanks for not firing me. Again."

"Maribelle would miss you." They stopped at the last step, and he turned to her. "You seem to have a way with her."

"Six-year-olds are easy."

His eyebrows shot up. "Oh, really?"

"Sure." She lifted one shoulder, let it drop. "At this age, all they want to do is be with you and know they're loved."

"Of course. And I do. Love her."

"And she loves you. She talks about you a lot."

He looked puzzled at that. Men. So clueless when it came to women—even the youngest kind.

They all shuffled outside, and instantly, the mood lifted. A photographer's light could never compete with the healing impact of real sunshine.

Ash and Maribelle were soon settled under the large tree in the center of Brickman Park. A smile finally formed on

Maribelle's face, and her dark curls danced in the soft breeze. The lighting made both of them glow. And their eyes? Like sapphires under a spotlight.

Ash seemed to absorb Maribelle's energy a bit, too. The lines across his forehead had eased, and his jaw wasn't doing that pulsing thing. He had such nice teeth. It'd be a shame to ruin them if he continued to grind them like he did.

He still ended up wearing his full suit, and Addy was not sorry about it.

The man could pose, too. Maybe *he* should have been a model. His jawline was dusted with a five o'clock shadow that had to be done by a stylist. No one grew anything that well on their own.

It was a shame he was so formal, and now that she studied his face, sad. She hadn't noticed that before. Then again, they'd not spent much time together where she could actually observe him.

Chief clapped his hands. "I think we've got it. That should do the trick."

Maribelle dropped her head dramatically on her father's shoulder. "Finally. I want some pie."

"We should celebrate," Addy declared. "Peppermint Sweet is across the street."

Ash glared at her. "No." He arched an eyebrow her way. Stern pirate face was back.

"They have sugar-free cupcakes. Though…" She stuck a finger in her mouth, the universal gagging motion. "They do have the best shade-grown coffee in town."

O'Connor stuffed his hands in his pockets. "It would be good for the locals to see you."

"The locals have seen enough of us."

Maribelle peered up at her father, her bottom lip jutted out. "But Daddy, what if I only have one bite?"

"We have things at home."

"Nothing good." She crossed her little arms and huffed.

Ash eased her down and stood. She refused to take his outstretched hand. He sent his gaze to the sky, then down to Chief. "You're joining us."

Ash's gaze then honed in on Addy. His eyes did that glittery thing like she was a rabbit in a forest and he was the hunter. He was not happy, but holy mother. If her underwear didn't slide down her legs at that moment it'd be a miracle because ensnare her now—please.

She took a big lungful of air to re-center and remind herself she was a nanny here to do a job. She'd gone into Ash Scott-overload, that was all. Any female would have this reaction after watching him in a suit for hours holding a little girl, getting completely undone by said child. It was pure science.

He was putting off that primal protector vibe.

He manufactured pheromones.

He was *suitnip*.

At least, that's what she continued to chant inside herself as she sat across from him in Peppermint Sweet at a little bistro table with the iron backs scrolled into hearts. She had to do something to quell her mind that had decided fantasizing about him was its new favorite pastime.

11

Ash wasn't supposed to be sitting alone with his nanny at this sugar palace. But as soon as they strode through the door of Peppermint Sweet, O'Connor, who'd been studying his phone the whole two-minute walk over, grabbed his arm. "Hold up. Something just came in. Be in there in a second."

Dammit, Ash had caved on visiting a bakeshop to do something nice for his daughter but chaperoned because this town had revealed itself. Like New York, it also had people dying to capture whatever story they could. Why hand it to them on a cupcake platter?

No matter what Adelaide said, the hometown Hamish guy wasn't harmless. Anyone who snuck onto private property to take pictures never was.

"Adelaide, mind getting something for Maribelle? No cupcakes. Something with real fruit."

The woman rolled her eyes. She had serious boss-employee boundary issues.

O'Connor finally sauntered inside and held up his phone screen to him. "The pictures from this morning. Already broke online. They're everywhere, but they're not bad."

"Not bad?"

He glanced at the screen. There was no mistaking the two of them in the picture. Adelaide with her mouth agape, clearly laughing. He was smiling back with a ridiculous water balloon in his hand. He scrubbed his hair. Pink. The balloon had to be pink.

He grabbed the phone and widened the screen. Goddammit, the frame included Maribelle. She was blurry and in the background, but still… Whatever happened to decency in this world, giving at least kids some privacy?

He glanced over at his daughter. She twirled in front of the young woman behind the counter. He recognized her from the farm visit pictures. The girl smiled down at Maribelle. They had a familiarity that made him uncomfortable. He didn't know that person, not really.

O'Connor lowered his phone. "Ash. It's only you, Maribelle, and Adelaide running around the backyard. It will blow over."

"You keep saying that."

The nanny chatted up the woman he now remembered as her sister. Wasn't that what she'd said? His insides chafed as the woman handed Maribelle a cone with something that most definitely didn't fit his no-sugar rule.

What had he expected coming into a bakeshop? His little girl had learned early how to get what she wanted, alright. Adelaide wasn't helping.

Chief widened his stance. "Adelaide might want to know about it. They haven't gone viral yet."

Yet. There was always a yet.

Adelaide looked happy in the picture. He did, too. But, dammit, the caption read, *'Ashton Scott's playdate with his nanny.'* What client would ever put their confidence in him again after this? Who would ever believe he'd changed if they happened upon those pictures? That he wasn't the guy who was seen with a different woman every night of his life? That he wasn't banging his nanny? Crude, but he knew how the masses quickly went to that place in their scandal-loving minds.

O'Connor held out his hand for his phone. "Listen, I'm going back to New York. I'll plant these pictures we took immediately."

"You're not leaving me with that woman." He pointed at Adelaide. "Now that the wrong idea about her has been put out into the world, the locals you're so fond of mentioning might think something."

Small-town gossip was more toxic than TMZ. If they spilled something to the gossip rags, their words had a certain credibility that a paparazzo's didn't.

The man had the gall to chuckle. "She won't bite. But if she does, give me a heads-up, okay? Before the headlines roll in?"

"There will be no headlines. You'll make sure of it, won't you? And there certainly will be no biting."

"You're a stronger man than me, Ashton Scott."

God, he wished he was. And right now, this man had no concept of how much he wanted to fire someone, including him if it meant he got to change something in his world.

It wouldn't help. And the man wasn't at fault here. He was. Time to fix things.

He ran his hand over his chin as O'Connor strode out, leaving him with one maverick nanny with questionable judgment and one little girl who was clearly besotted with her.

His phone pinged and one glance showed O'Connor had sent him the picture. For what? A souvenir as the only fun he'd had in… hell, couldn't even count the years. Maybe since… Kate. That night they'd been together had been something different. They'd laughed, talked trash about the other socialites, made love on the balcony of her suite with the innocent thought if anyone saw they'd wish they could be one of them.

So naïve. But he'd gone willingly. And just like Kate, Adelaide had a way of worming her way under his control.

He took in a few breaths, told himself to be smart about approaching his situation this time.

He strode up to the counter.

Maribelle held up a cone filled with pastry pieces and a rich blueberry filling. "Daddy, want some?"

"No, thanks." He looked over at Adelaide. "I trust that's sugar-free?" He attempted to keep his tone light for his daughter's sake.

Her eyebrows lifted. "Low-sugar? You said no cupcakes, just fruit."

He had. "Espresso, please," he said to the woman behind the counter. Her name tag read Scarlett. "Two shots."

"Coming right up." She waggled her eyebrows and then sent her gaze to Adelaide. "A 15," Scarlett said.

Fifteen dollars?

Adelaide held up both hands. "Don't listen to my sister."

"Yes, I remember you saying you were sisters."

"Yep."

They looked nothing alike. Scarlett had a riot of blond curly hair that spilled down a peasant blouse, and Adelaide had hair as dark as his espresso and bright, shining blue-gray eyes that stared at you like she was drinking you in.

Maribelle jumped up and down and tugged at his suit-coat. "Scarlett said she can show me how she makes the animal cookies. Can I, Daddy? Can I go see how to make animal cookies?"

"She offered for Maribelle to use the big cut-outs on the dough." Adelaide pointed to a large, white swinging door. "Inside that door. And for the record, they are the least sugary thing on the menu. Scarlett's arm is as good as mine, so no one will get near Maribelle. I promise."

Funny she'd know exactly where he'd go in his mind with that one. He didn't like having Maribelle out of his sight.

Scarlett cocked her head back and forth. "Debatable. I think I'm better. Like, this one time with one of our stallions. Oh, my God, he thought he could pull—"

He raised his hand to stop another litany of words. These two were most definitely sisters.

Maribelle's eyes grew round, pleading. "Please, Daddy?"

Fuck him. He glanced around. The shop was practically empty. "Okay, but we can't stay long. Adelaide and I will be here. We need to… talk."

Maribelle grabbed Scarlett's hand, her pie cone in her other hand. Yet another stranger she seemed to trust.

"Let's sit." He gestured to the small bistro table at the front window.

Addy set the coffee and tea down. "I'm surprised you let her go. But thank you."

Thanking him? "She deserves to have fun." Just not in front of a photographer.

Addy nodded and blew on her tea.

He picked up his coffee. "I'm not the ogre that you think I am." Why was he explaining himself to her?

"I don't think that." She quickly glanced back down at her tea.

"Listen, that photographer from this morning—"

"Yeah, Hamish."

A loud knock sounded on the glass. Sally Albrecchio's bright smile beamed in on them. She waved like a lunatic then pointed at the front door and nodded. The universal signal of *I'm joining you whether I was invited or not.* Oh, great.

The woman was by their table in seconds.

"Why, look who it is." Sally beamed at him.

"It's Sally," Adelaide said a little too brightly.

The woman's face stretched wide. "And it's Nanny Bloom."

Female rivalry, Jesus.

She returned her attention to Ash. "I've been meaning to stop by your place. I have some books for you… to help prepare Maribelle for school." She glanced up at Adelaide again. "I have a feeling you could use the help." Sally glanced around. "Where is the little princess, by the way?"

"Queen Maribelle is making cookies," Adelaide interjected quickly. "In the back."

"Oh, so she is here. That's good. I mean, you wouldn't want anyone to get the wrong idea here." She waved her hand back and forth between Ash and Addy. She held up her phone. "There have been some pictures showing up today. Anyway, I'll drop those books off to you. Let you both be for now."

She'd seen the pictures. The news had moved at warp speed.

He and Adelaide both watched Sally traipse through the door, the bell over the door tinkling a good-bye.

Adelaide turned her gaze to him. "Pictures already? From the water balloon fight?" She leaned back and started laughing like a hyena. "Oh, my God. Who cares what we were doing? Hamish… get a life."

His sentiments exactly. "It doesn't look good."

She shook her head. "But so what if we were running around your backyard? It's your life. Unless…" She lifted her gaze to him. "Do I look fat? Did he get me making a horse face or something? I looked like a horse, didn't I? I'll kill him."

An unexpected laugh threatened to rise up. "That's what you're worried about? How you look?"

"Spoken like a man who looks like… like… you." She lifted a hand toward him.

"Well, you could never look… like a horse." She couldn't, if he was honest. "But Ms. Albrecchio is on the board of the academy and she mustn't get the wrong idea."

"Mustn't?" She rolled her lips between her teeth as if holding in some amusement.

"No. She. Mustn't."

Adelaide twisted her cup in her saucer. "Well, it is true she will take any opportunity to stick it to someone. Don't I know it." She snorted, lifted her cup, and took a sip of tea. Her brow suddenly pinched, and she set the cup down with a loud clink. "You know what? Screw all those people. You're a good father. No one can take that away from you with a bunch of pictures that show you having fun with your daughter. If anything, it makes you look good." She nodded once sharply.

His shoulders dropped an inch. She'd done it again. Caught him off-guard. But every bit of trouble in his life had come from a surprise—except for Maribelle.

"Thank you. But perception is everything, I'm afraid, and Maribelle's privacy is critical." He took a sip of his espresso. It was good. Very good. "I can't let this negatively impact her."

"See? All you're worried about is her. Like I said. A good father."

He ran a finger over his chin. He was trying to be.

"Don't let Sally get to you. She has always viewed herself as someone who is better than this town and everyone in it."

"This town isn't for everyone."

"There's a difference between something not fitting you and thinking it's something beneath you. Guess which camp she falls into."

He understood that one. It hit a little too close to home. "You and she have a past?"

"She doesn't like me." She shrugged. "I'm not everyone's cup of tea." She looked thoughtful. "I'm more of a hibiscus chamomile mix while Sally is more…"

"Yes?" He was far too interested in her answer.

"A black tea that's been steeped too long. Be warned. Sally wants to date you."

He doubted that. Sally wanted to be near a spotlight. "I don't date."

"Never?" Her eyebrows shot up to her hairline.

He didn't answer. What would he say? He'd had his share of women up north, but now, not only did he not have time but his inclination had also dropped off the second he met his daughter. It was like he didn't know how to determine who might fit with *her*.

And then the fortune-hunters had begun to swarm around him like bees seeking a new hive—a gold-plated one.

It was easier to focus on the two tasks at hand—work and Maribelle.

Adelaide waved her hand. "I shouldn't have asked that."

"It's okay. But if there is anything I need to know about you and Sally, you'll fill me in. I mean, she's on the girl's academy board…" He waited for her to fill him in. She didn't.

Adelaide sat back, letting the silence fill between them.

"There's something you're not saying." He couldn't let it sit. He had a little girl to think about.

"I'd rather not talk about it. It's… private."

He leaned back in the chair, the iron scrollwork pressing uncomfortably on his body. "Is it anything that might make Sally view Maribelle… differently?"

Her lips thinned. "Because of me. Because I watch over her."

A hard lump formed in his chest. Having to say what

needed to be said shouldn't be hard here. Somehow, the words weren't coming to him, however. He stared down at his espresso, studying the foam lining the little cup. "Your probation term is coming up for discussion."

"Oh. I see."

He glanced up just as she shoved herself against the back of the chair.

"I need to decide what's best for my daughter."

Her face hardened. She took another sip of tea. "If you believe I'm not suitable to take care of Maribelle, I trust you'll do the right thing."

"I meant…"

She scraped her chair backward, and Maribelle bounced over with a cookie in each hand. She also was chewing. "I got to make the monkeys."

Adelaide beamed down at her—and Maribelle smiled back.

"Let's go." He rose and pulled Maribelle up into his arms. She pushed a cookie toward his mouth, and he shook his chin. "You've had enough. Leave them here."

Her mouth went slack, a sheen of tears forming in her eyes. "But I made them."

"Hey, can I have a bite?" Adelaide put her hand on Maribelle's back.

Maribelle snuffed up her nose and handed one of the cookies over to her.

Adelaide bit into it and made too-loud happy noises. "You made a great cookie, Queen Maribelle."

His little girl reached both arms over toward the nanny.

He let her go. He'd made Maribelle cry—twice. Made her suffer through O'Connor's plans, something he'd sworn he left New York to get away from. And now? He couldn't stop being an ass.

It was the damn photographers—and now, a potential,

long-standing rift between the next chair of the girl's academy and his nanny. He was so done with two steps forward, three steps back.

He gestured toward the door, and thankfully, Adelaide followed without a word.

The car ride home was then the longest she'd gone without talking since he'd met her.

12

Ash hovered outside Maribelle's room. Adelaide had been spinning a bedtime story. Something about pirates and faraway lands with trees with leaves made of spun sugar. He stayed tucked in the shadow the half-open door threw into the hallway.

Adelaide pulled the blanket up higher over Maribelle. "And then the princess knew she had to save herself."

Maribelle's little fingers worked the ribbon on her favorite doll that was tucked by her side. "She killed the evil Queen Sally?"

"Nah." Adelaide waved her hand. "She bested her. That's always better." Addy tapped Maribelle's nose. "She got her em-bee-ay, built a beautiful castle on the sea, and invited all the stray animals to live with her. It was the best life ever."

Maribelle gasped. "And horses?"

"Lots of horses, and even some ostriches."

Maribelle giggled.

"You know your grandmother loved ostriches?"

"She did?" Her eyes grew round. His probably did, too. His mother loving any animal? Hardly.

"Yep. She used to come to our farm and feed ours."

What was this woman talking about? Come to think of it, his mother did have this hat with these long feathers stuck in them. Jesus, what would he know? His ears craned to hear more when Adelaide dropped her voice.

"She loved Bouncy Boy the best because he used to do this bouncy dance thing. Especially when he saw her."

"I didn't meet them the other day."

"Sadly, we don't have them anymore. They went to live in Ostrich Heaven."

"Like my grandma."

He nearly shot himself into the room. How did Maribelle know that? Had Kate known his parents? No, she couldn't have. Maribelle probably deduced it given no grandparents had greeted them at the door when they'd first arrived. Why hadn't he thought of talking to her about his parents, how they'd passed some time ago within three days of each other? Oh, maybe he hadn't mentioned anything because this nanny apparently knew more about them than he did.

Maribelle's eyes caught Ash hovering in the doorway. "Daddy, you're going to build me a castle soon, right? Then I can have my animal friends come over. I want an ostrich."

Adelaide lifted her gray eyes his way. No smile formed on her face. He thought her smiles were too much? Not seeing one was worse.

He pushed off the doorframe. "Soon on the castle. I promise."

Adelaide rose and left the space she once occupied for him. He knelt down. "Thanks for being such a good girl today, And I'm sorry I yelled earlier."

"It's okay, Daddy, you just need some of Addy's magic oil. It calms the soul."

He let out a half-laugh. "I'll have to try that sometime. Now, it's time for dreamland." He tucked the covers around her a little tighter. "You got Mary Catherine Louisa March and Prickly Puss all settled?"

"Yep. Prickly Puss is on guard duty tonight." She always had to line up her dolls around her like a protection shield.

At that moment, Ash looked up at Adelaide and instantly caught something in Adelaide's eyes—an understanding. Perhaps Maribelle had told her the story of the break-in in New York. Why he wouldn't think she'd keep it to herself, he'd never know. Except Maribelle had not wanted to talk about her mother or what had happened ever since they were put together a year ago.

Then again, Adelaide had a way of drawing things out of people, especially his daughter. Safety—wasn't that what a good nanny produced? Only, with what little he knew of her, he walked a balance beam of believing her instincts and desiring to put a body camera on her 24/7.

Man, his time in Manhattan had split him in two, but his suspicions of everyone around him had served him well, and his own instincts were screaming bloody murder like yet another shoe was about to drop.

He pressed a kiss to Maribelle's forehead. "Goodnight, sweetheart."

Maribelle immediately closed her eyes, likely exhausted from the day—or she was undergoing a sugar crash.

He glanced up at Adelaide. "Let's talk downstairs."

She blinked at him but wisely questioned no further.

Adelaide put on the small night-light that sent images of butterflies flying around the room.

Together, they walked out.

Just outside the door, he turned to her. "Care to have dinner with me? Downstairs, of course. It's a bit lonely sitting in that dining room by myself." He'd waited far too long to fill Adelaide in completely. Local man or not, the photographers had found them. Why did he think they wouldn't? She now needed to know why it was so bad.

"Sure. I forgot how big this house is." She looked around. "I used to hate to be here by myself when it got dark. All the shadows."

He nodded. "Monsters around every corner, if I recall." Now, however, real monsters existed in the shadows. Tonight, Adelaide would learn why photographers tracking their every move was akin to death—and why Maribelle felt the need for guard dolls.

13

———————

The giant grandfather clock ticked into the silence. Adelaide twisted her napkin in her lap and tried not to stare at Ash across the formal dining room. She was failing at that miserably, of course. She kept sneaking glances at him.

She was rapidly becoming one of Ashton Scott's swoon-gang. She didn't know if it existed, but it had to. The man was designed to be stared at—even testy, like today. In fact, he made anger look hot.

Oh, she was pissed at him for being such an oaf earlier, but her anger cooled at seeing him trying so hard to make amends with Maribelle. The little girl thoroughly thawed his prickly, freezy face, which only made him dishier.

He set his fork down. "Everything alright?"

Addy dropped her chin. "I was admiring the woodwork."

She'd been studying every inch of the familiar room, again thinking it'd take her mind off his mouth, his neck when he swallowed. It didn't. The man even chewed brussels sprouts sexily. And that was saying something.

He twiddled with the stem of his wine glass. "My mother loved this room, apparently."

She didn't think the Scott family ever used this room, but then again, she'd never been here when "the family," as her mother called them, ate dinner. "She told me every part of this house spoke to her."

"Spoke to her, huh?"

"Yep. It said, 'Dust me.' So that's what I did—a lot." She took a sip of her water.

He laughed. He had a good one. He should use it more often. "About that." He adjusted in his seat as if uncomfortable. "You said we once met. Can you jog my memory?"

She stuck her hands under her thighs. "Maybe?"

He lifted his napkin and dabbed the side of his mouth but then dropped it again in his lap. Waited. This was how he got people to talk in the courtroom, wasn't it? He kept his beautiful lips closed and stared at yours with those wholly-unfair weapons called his blue eyes. The sky over a still ocean couldn't be as clear blue.

He cocked his head. "Well?"

She should tell him. It's just she'd worked hard at stuffing down the day they'd met. She'd been successful until a week ago when he unexpectedly jettisoned his way back into her purview.

Plus, she was on probation as he'd brought up today. Obviously, he was thinking of letting her go. Why push herself out the front door by admitting what had happened between them? She loved this job. She wanted to keep it despite his very presence being one hell of a distraction. "It wasn't a big deal. I was fourteen. You were seventeen."

He pushed his empty plate away. "Ah, seventeen. That would put me at my biggest asshole stage, I believe."

She blinked. She hadn't expected such self-awareness. "Most guys at that time were like you. I was an easy target. I grew up *unusually*."

"What do you mean by target?"

He didn't want to know all this, did he? What could she tell him? That her family were the black sheep of Moorsville? Farmers who took anything in with fur—or scales.

Then there was the time her father thought he could make a killing by growing truffles. Even bought the pig who could only find its way to her mother's kitchen door. It didn't help her mother was constantly throwing it apples.

Or her mother's obsession with herbs and thought she was a "green witch." Tried to sell her herbed bath salts under the name of Bloom Bombs at the Saturday morning Moorsville street fair.

Then there were her mother's outfits. She had a penchant for big, floppy hats and cropped pants with animal patterns. Not just any animals, though. Pumas and sloths were her favorites. She enjoyed the polar opposites, Addy supposed.

She swallowed. "I'm surprised you don't know about my family. I mean, given you grew up here."

"I visited here. I didn't exactly have the typical Moorsville life."

"You should be glad. Instead, you got a great career. Penthouses. Supermodels…" she waved her hand.

"You are a little obsessed with the supermodel thing. You've mentioned it a few times."

How could she forget, staring at his supermodel-in the-making daughter? "Well, I always knew you were destined for big things. You told me so."

His eyebrows shot to his hairline. "I did?"

She pushed her own plate away. "But now, you and Maribelle are here. Not New York. And you wanted to fill me in on some things?" She'd much rather hear about him than dredge up that one and only night they'd met.

"Yes. Our last few months in New York were challenging. I suppose you read the headlines."

"Some."

"There's a lot that was kept out of the press thanks to Chief."

That was the first time she'd heard him refer to Chief O'Connor by his first name. He seemed inordinately fond of last names. "You two are friends."

He angled his head. "I wouldn't say that. More like mutually respectful of one another. He does a good job for me."

"Even if he makes you touch tree bark."

"Even so. Better still, he kept quite a bit quiet. Like why Maribelle…" He visibly swallowed.

"Why she has guard dolls?"

"Has she told you anything? About what happened before we got here?"

"She doesn't talk about her old life much." Adelaide was surprised about that. She must have inherited Ash's ability to stuff everything down because that was most definitely one of his tactics. She didn't need a psychology degree to ferret out that characteristic.

He threw back the last of his wine and set the glass down a little forcefully. "She's justified in being scared. When her mother died, news of her inheritance was leaked. Lots of press. Then someone broke into our apartment when I wasn't home."

Adelaide gasped a little.

His hand found its way to the knife by his empty plate. "The doorman showed up with a package. Found the door open and was suspicious. He found a woman in Maribelle's room. When the police arrived, they found a roll of duct tape in her bag. But just the woman's presence alone scared Maribelle to the core."

Adelaide was unable to keep her lips from falling open. Flamethrowers lit up her legs and she shot to standing. "How did she get in? What about the nanny? Didn't she or he protect Maribelle?"

"The nanny was in on it. That's how the woman got in."

"What?" She slammed both hands on the table, making the cutlery ring. "But Practically Perfect Nannies—"

"She wasn't from that agency. She was recommended to me by someone."

Adelaide slowly lowered herself back to her seat. "And now this nanny is being chased around a jail cell by someone named Big Martha?" Or worse. A huge lump formed in her throat, and she fought like hell to not cry. Now, Maribelle hiding in the closet and having her dolls all around her when she slept made perfect sense. No child should ever have to *fortress* for real.

She threw herself against the back of the chair and hugged her middle as if that might help hold in the wail that wanted to break out.

"I appreciate your enthusiastic sentiment." He didn't sound excited. His voice was flat, or perhaps he was holding in a rage that she herself was struggling with keeping contained. "So, that's why it's important we know who is in this household at all times."

"Consider that *done*. I can punch more than fish, you know. Not that I'm a violent person, but this girl?" She pointed at her chest. "She has an arm on her. You've seen it."

His eyes shone at her. "Yes, I have." His face stilled. "But it will take more than a water balloon, I'm afraid. Maribelle has assets. Things other people want."

She knew that, thanks to Scarlett. Everything started to click into place like tumblers in a lock. "I'm surprised you left her with me that first day. In the agency office."

"I trusted you for some reason." He lowered his chin. "Maybe I could tell you had a good arm."

She smiled at him but sobered instantly. What he and Maribelle had been through was unconscionable. "That's why you're in Moorsville, isn't it? Because it's safer."

"That's one reason. I always found this place to be exceedingly quiet."

She snuffled out a laugh. "Well, I guess, compared to New York, yes." This town, however, had its own hidden perils.

His hand worried the handle of his knife. "But you don't find it that way?"

She was shocked he was asking so many questions about her. But he'd seen the worst of the worst, right? And now the man had to be scared for his daughter. Perhaps he'd learned to live with the past she'd just now gotten privy to.

She leaned forward and placed her elbows on the table. "It's safe, meaning I seriously doubt anyone is going to show up with duct tape. But, like all small towns, everyone's up in everyone else's business. And… well, you're a bit of a magnet. I mean, expect people to be curious about you and your life. You're a celebrity here. Like, take Sally, for instance…"

The words had tumbled out before she could stuff them back into her throat and gag on them. But she couldn't see Maribelle traumatized anymore—and Sally had a way of bruising marble statues when she got too close. The idea of Sally getting a foothold in this house made her want to hurl the Scott china plate before her against the wall.

Ash eyed her. "About Sally. What's up there?"

She was going to have to tell him something, wasn't she? "Okay, you told me your secrets, now I'll tell you something about me." She raised her hands "But I promise it's nothing truly horrible." Liar. "Unless… How good is your sense of humor?"

He arched an eyebrow in answer. As if she needed him to confirm that he was very good at choking that down as well.

The pertinent parts were all that was needed. "I was once engaged to her younger brother."

"Ah." A smile broke onto his face. "You broke his heart, and she didn't like it."

If only it was that simple. "No. He broke it off with me. She never approved of me anyway. I think part of it is I was adopted."

"That's not a reason to dislike someone."

"It is for her. She's from one of the oldest families here."

"So am I. Where you came from doesn't mean anything about your character. I knew you were adopted, and you're here. Yes, I Googled you, too." He winked at her, which about made her slide off her chair. For one, she didn't think Ashton Scott winked. And another thing, he'd looked her up.

What did she expect? He was leery of people he didn't know. That was all. It didn't mean he was interested in her. He didn't have dreams about her.

Oh, my holy… Did he?

No. He didn't imagine…

Smutty, eager, and wholly delusional mind, please, take a rest.

"So?" He let the question hang in the air.

She couldn't do it, couldn't tell him everything that would change the way he was looking at her now. He was being so… human with her. She didn't want to risk him thinking she was a monster and see him put up a shield on his face again.

Thank God when her and Bryson's break-up occurred, no one thought to actually post online what she'd done in retaliation. Recording what was going on around you wasn't a favorite pastime, unlike now. People were still posting what they had for breakfast back then. Nothing like today.

Ash had both of his hands curled around the table edge. At least he'd dropped the knife. "But it is interesting to me that your sister and you look about the same age."

His suspicions were still on fire. "We are. Six months apart. My parents found out they were pregnant three days after bringing me home. Surprise! I have to give them credit for not giving me back."

His chin jutted back. "I would think not."

"Well… It was suggested by more than a few people. In fact, it was Sally who told me I was adopted in third grade." She rubbed her sternum remembering that day. Sally, the older girl who thought wearing lipstick by age fifteen made her grown-up, sniffing down at Addy who'd been playing with her brother on the playground.

"Why would she do that?"

"Who knows? She was one of the town's snobby girl's academy squad. But it's a small town and we ran into each other all the time." She had to shake off that memory. "Anyway, until that point, my sister and I thought we were twins. That's what our parents told us. I think it was their way of making us believe we were equals." She laughed a little.

"You're close to your sister. The one you can't say 'no' to."

"Very. But she's more resilient than me. You know," she put her elbows on the table "…Maribelle is resilient too. She is going to be fine. And I meant what I said at Peppermint Sweet. You're doing a good job with her. Even when you sometimes use your mad voice."

"If only I knew that to be true."

Finally, she saw an "in," something to reduce his angst. "Look, I've been with twenty-seven families, as you know. I've seen stuff. She's quite advanced in some ways, in other ways not. But that's totally normal at her age."

"It does seem you know a lot about kids. When it's your turn to have them—"

"Oh, no. I'm meant to be a nanny." She swallowed and prayed he wouldn't ask her any more questions. She was not sure she'd have the strength to not answer.

They'd dredged up enough of the past for one night.

He continued to stare at her. "You do have a good sense of yourself. I wish that for Maribelle."

"She does, and she's very creative. Like how she uses her

dolls to self-soothe, and wow, she can read a lot." She took another sip of water.

"Thanks, Adelaide. I appreciate you telling me that."

"I imagine people are afraid to tell you things. But not me. You *are* doing a great job."

Finally, he smiled.

"Even if you won't let her eat pie." She couldn't help herself.

"Something tells me she's going to be eating pie while you are around."

"Well, I took a look at that new Genius book you sent me."

"I'm impressed you looked at it at all."

She shrugged "I was bored one night. You don't have cable. And honestly, it's not so bad even though there are quite a few things in it that make *no* sense."

He harumphed but didn't seem angry—for once. "Such as?"

"The brain needs glucose, you know."

"Fruit."

"Pie is fruit." She raised a finger. "And plain fruit is not nearly as much fun."

"Fun isn't the only goal of life."

Man, he'd lived an uptight life. Knowing his mother, how did this happen? His mom snuck her cookies and told her grand stories of dancing with her grandfather in the old hotels in New York City. She'd even said she'd take Addy one day. She didn't, but still… "Don't you ever let it all hang out? I mean, even play golf?"

"No."

"Well, anytime you want to have a water balloon fight, which I believe is cathartic, let me know. Unless you think you'll lose again." She couldn't help ribbing him. Making his grumpy face twitch was kind of fun. And, honestly, keeping one's face frozen wasn't healthy. His facial muscles might forget how to smile.

"More water balloons? My, my." Sally stood in the doorway.

Just when Addy thought she was rid of this woman, she kept appearing like an unwanted rash. Addy's skin certainly prickled as if one was forming.

Sally beamed her smiled at Ash, then sent her gaze over the dinner set for two, lingering on the empty wine bottle. "Oh, how cozy."

Sally was no dummy. She took in every molecule in the room and rearranged them in her head into a story that would sound the best at her whine-fests disguised as a book club. Ash had no idea how screwed he was in that moment.

But Addy did.

Hello, high school. I haven't missed you one bit.

14

Ash nearly toppled his chair backward standing up. "Ms. Albrecchio, is there something I can do for you?"

"I didn't mean to interrupt your dinner." She held an armful of books. "The door was cracked wide open and…"

His door was sealed, but what could he do? Kick her out? "Please, come in. Can I get you something to drink? We were just finished."

"Oh, no. I was only dropping these off. Like I said I would this afternoon." She trooped inside and set the books next to Adelaide, who had risen from her seat—more like shot up as if fired from a canon.

"Mr. Scott, I should go check on Maribelle."

Adelaide learned fast, adding that bit of formality to the scene. He appreciated it. "Thank you, Miss Bloom." He was having a good time with her, amazingly, as if they were any two people having dinner, getting to know one another. Sally didn't need to know that.

Adelaide tried to scoot by, but Sally grasped her arm. "You recognize these, don't you, Adelaide?"

"I recognize a lot of things." She then freed herself and marched toward the door.

Adelaide had not told him her and Sally's whole story, that was for certain. She might have if they hadn't been interrupted.

Adelaide paused in the doorway and twisted back to face them.

"You should know Mr. Scott is a terrific father. He does everything by the book already." She glanced down at the stack of paperbacks. "But I wouldn't recommend the top one. It does psychological damage to tell a child, or anyone for that matter, that there's only one way to live—your way."

"My, you certainly have opinions, don't you?" Sally tittered a little as if trying to make light of the situation.

Adelaide's right eye twitched, probably suppressing an eye roll. He was rather amused by it—when it wasn't aimed at him.

"Adelaide, I'll see you upstairs when I go to check on Maribelle in a bit." The minute the words came out of his mouth, he knew they were the wrong things to utter in front of Sally. She had seen the photographs, after all. "Upstairs" implied too much.

If, however, she'd noticed he'd let Adelaide's informal address slip—using her first name—Sally didn't let on.

The woman stepped forward another foot. "I also came by to ask you something." She continued to inch closer to him, and her perfume crashed in on him again. "I wondered if you'd like to go to this art gallery opening with me. It's a local gallery filled with local artists. Probably not anything remotely close to what you see in New York, but I find it's important to support the community."

He sent his gaze back to her, not realizing his eyes had locked on Adelaide as she'd sashayed out.

Sally cocked her head. "Unless…" She peered behind her

toward where Adelaide had disappeared. "…you're otherwise occupied."

Good time or not, he wouldn't have her get the wrong idea. "No. Not occupied. What evening?" With any luck, at least a local photographer would see them together and without a nanny in sight. Maybe he'd extend an invitation to that Hamish fellow. Even pose for the fucker.

"Tuesday. Six p.m. cocktails."

"I'd be delighted. I haven't been out and about very much."

"Wonderful, I can meet you there or…" She left the space open. He knew this game. Adelaide may have been right about her romantic interest. She wanted to be picked up. He needed Maribelle to get a good start at the girl's academy but he had no intention of leading this woman on.

"I'll meet you there."

She touched his arm. He worked hard at not flinching. "I'll text you. Then you'll have my number."

Oh, he had her number alright, and she probably swiped his from Maribelle's application.

He saw her out and then took the stairs up, two at a time. He found Adelaide gently closing Maribelle's door in the darkened hallway. Shadows and light from the one small lamp on a nearby table cast geometric patterns on the carpet and walls.

She held a finger to her lips, then walked right up to him. "You're being played."

Jesus. Get to the point, will you? "You overheard Sally's offer."

"Offer?" She scoffed. "She's manipulating you."

He knew that, but he had to earn the right perception of him in this town. He wouldn't let Maribelle's future be tainted by any salacious gossip about him banging the nanny. Crude, but he knew how people's minds worked. If one evening drinking lukewarm chardonnay in a room filled with B-rated paintings helped his daughter, he'd do it.

What he didn't understand was how Adelaide couldn't understand the situation. Unless… "And you would know about this manipulation because?" If she had more to say, she should spill it.

"Because I know Sally." She lifted her chin and set her jaw.

He stepped closer. "Is that all? What aren't you telling me?"

Dead silence greeted him.

He exhaled a long breath. "No words. How interesting."

"What does that mean?" A meteor shower had nothing on the fiery sparks in her eyes. She didn't yield the field easily. He liked that about her. She had grit.

But so did he. "I don't care what you and Sally have going on. As for me and Sally? You should have no opinion about it whatsoever."

"I know people around here and, well, I do have opinions."

"I don't want them." Affinity notwithstanding, her history couldn't impact him or Maribelle.

What he did know about their shared past whirred through his brain. The brother dumps her. Sally probably gloated about it. She seemed to be a woman who'd do such a thing. Perhaps all Adelaide wanted was a little retribution for being mistreated. He felt bad for her if that was the case, but he didn't have time for this small-town crap.

The game, at least in this house, had to end. "We're slipping into too much informality between us. We need to button things back up… or…"

He'd fire her? Break Maribelle's heart?

Her throat moved in a tight swallow. She wanted to say something. Her whole face lit up with unspoken words.

They stood like that for long seconds, staring at one another in the darkened hallway.

It strangely made him want to yank her closer, close his hand around the back of her neck, and help loosen that tension. *Fuck*, why was that coming up? Because he liked her. She was interesting. Real. He didn't find many interesting, real people. Hell, he didn't *like* many people period.

He dropped his gaze to his shoes, more to break whatever spell she was casting on him than to yield the field.

"Do what you need to do," she finally hissed out. "I mean, I'm on probation, right? And it's your rules. Your house. Your daughter. I'm nobody."

Why was she reacting so strongly to this? *Hell*, why was he?

He sighed. He needed to level her expectations. "I am paying you to help Maribelle make a good first impression at a school she will be entering in less than two weeks."

"A good impression for her or you?"

"Jesus. No wonder you've been with twenty-seven families."

All emotion in her face drained. Her eyes shone a little too much.

Fuck him. "We're calling it a night. You're welcome to crash again in one of the guest bedrooms." They could pick it up in the morning.

"I plan on it. For Maribelle's sake." She spun on her heel and disappeared down to the darker end of the hallway.

Jesus, she was stubborn. Cagey. Maddening. And yeah, smart. Not wholly wrong about the situation but not exactly helping it, either.

She also was entirely too appealing. Watching her slip through her bedroom door? His legs vibrated, wanting to follow.

Dammit. She'd started to interest him, and she'd gained

Maribelle's trust—and his—faster than he'd expected. He'd relaxed quite a few things in a matter of days because of this woman.

He had to get a handle on this situation. She was entirely too invested too fast, that's what this was. It was going to be a problem.

15

———————

Addy scratched her arm for the hundredth time. She itched all over despite the fact that she nestled under pure Egyptian cotton bedsheets that had to have had at least a 1000 thread count.

Nothing too good for Ashton Scott. The Exalted One. Moorsville's most eligible bachelor. The arrogant, sugar-hating, lumberyard-up-his-butt worry wort. The man, who despite said crankiness, had icy blue eyes that made her a walking bag of turned-on hormones. The man who might fire her all because of Sally.

Damn that woman and her covert hostile ways. Ash had let her get to him twice now. So disappointing. He was better than that. *Smarter* than that.

She threw off the cover and swung her legs over the side of the bed. She wasn't getting anywhere in the sleep department. Queen Maribelle was sure to come bounding in at sunup. Addy needed tea. A nice cup of chamomile would do the trick.

She padded down the wide staircase. The chime of an old, wall-hung grandfather clock sounded a metronome beat into the still house. She swung open the kitchen door and skidded to a stop.

Ash leaned against the counter, a coffee cup to his lips. He swung his gaze to her and immediately straightened. He opened his lips to speak but then snapped them shut.

Steeling her spine, she marched inside. "Just getting some tea." She opened a cabinet. It was the wrong one, of course. The shelves were filled with bowls and plates.

"Purple hibiscus?"

What do you know? He'd been listening at Peppermint Sweet. When he wasn't thinking about letting her go. "Chamomile." She opened another cabinet. This one contained water glasses.

Her eyes glanced over to where Ash slid open a drawer. "I believe this is what you're seeking."

Seeking. The man talked like a dictionary. "Yes. Seeking." She reached over and pulled out the chamomile teabag.

He ambled over to the electric kettle and pressed the button. He pulled a mug out of a different cabinet. Now the man was being helpful?

He cleared his throat. "I'm sorry."

Her blood froze. Right now would be a good time for her to be the bigger person, or at least, meet him halfway. Then why couldn't she turn to face him?

How about because on the heels of an apology, one look in his twinkling eyes and her defenses would turn to ash, like his name. Maybe his name was truly the universal warning sign she should learn to heed. She'd be nothing but cinders around him eventually.

Unlike his daughter, she didn't know how to "fortress"— not when it came to this man who had inched so close to her his warmth threatened to suffocate her last shred of composure.

"Truly sorry," he said slowly.

She twisted so her back was against the counter edge, and when her eyes found his, she might have forgotten to breathe. Yep, cinders and ash.

"Ash…" She'd whispered his name.

He moved impossibly closer. "Yes?"

You know what? She also was right about how he smelled. Totally expensive men's store with a hint of leather, wool, and some spicy concoction that was probably the number one pheromone guaranteed to lure supermodels to his bed.

She curled her hands around the edge of the granite counter. "Is it okay if I call you Ash?"

"You may. Since we met before."

She flushed from head to toe. "Then you should call me Addy."

One side of his mouth lifted. "Baby steps. How about Adelaide?"

"That works, too."

The tea kettle began to rumble. "I'm sorry, too, for my earlier… tension."

He dipped his chin once.

She swallowed. "I know things haven't been easy for you and Maribelle. You don't have to worry about me… jutting in where I'm not wanted." There, bigger person.

"I wouldn't say it's not wanted."

"I'm used to it. Like I said, I'm not everyone's cuppa."

"Like Sally's."

She sighed as the old arrows still lodged in her chest ached. They just couldn't get away from her, could they? "Like Sally. She gets to me." And clearly him. "She had a hand in my… the whole breakup thing with Bryson. Anyway, I know how hard it must be, I mean, to lose someone you cared about."

Understanding shone from his eyes. "Kate and I were just

friends. I'm sorry she's gone, but I feel mostly for Maribelle. And if Sally Albrecchio could come between you and your fiancée, I'd question his ability to be a good husband."

Addy released the grip on the counter and let them drop to her sides. "See? You had to go say something perfect like that and…"

"And what?"

Why not speak the truth? "You're going to make some woman's dream, ya' know? Someone *not* the town's busybody."

He scrubbed his chin. "I'm not anyone's dream."

"You're…" Whoops. She'd almost voiced something she should *never*. It was his blue eyes. They were truth serum. "Maribelle's dream. She's guaranteed to compare every man to you."

"God help her," he laughed. "I just hope she has standards."

She mock-punched his arm, her knuckles hitting solid muscle. She tried hard not to notice it too much. "Don't worry. I'll make sure she knows there's only one Ashton Scott. She'll have to find someone else." She let out a relieved breath. They were having a normal conversation again. "And if you need me to, I can take Sally."

"I'll bet you could." His eyes crinkled. "But you don't exactly have a mean streak in you."

"How do you know?"

He tapped his forehead. "I know things."

The tea kettle hissed loudly and the beeper went off. Still smiling, he reached over to it and poured the hot water into the mug. He pushed it toward her, and she spun to face it, finally able to rip her gaze from the man. She dropped a tea bag into the water and pretended to be uber-fascinated by the little simmer it made hitting the hot liquid.

He leaned against the counter, putting his silhouette in

her vision again. Even the rising chamomile scent and steam couldn't compete with how good he smelled. He still wore his shirt and dress pants. Did the man even own a pair of jeans?

He cleared his throat. "But seriously, I know people. I've seen the meanest of the mean, the most selfish of the selfish. You're none of those things."

A warmth settled in her chest. If only he knew. Pushed hard enough, even Adelaide Bloom could do something terrible. "Thank you. That's the nicest thing anyone has said to me in a long time."

"It wasn't that big of a compliment."

"It was to me. I mean, coming from you. You're The Exalted One."

He rolled his eyes. "That ridiculous article."

She lifted the cup to her lips and blew on the steam. "It wasn't ridiculous."

He sobered. "What did I do… when I was seventeen?"

This man truly was an attorney. He could ferret out a half-truth when he heard it, perhaps. Like the one she'd told him at dinner. "You don't want to know."

"That bad, huh?" He drew closer, dang it all.

She waved her hand. "You told me you were headed to great things."

"And?"

He was going to make him tell her, wasn't he? "You said… 'Unlike you.'"

He rose to his full height. "I did not." He eyed her. "Did I really?"

"Well, there was a bit more." She turned to the counter and set her too-hot mug down. "I-I told you how much I admired you." She studied a chip in the paint on the cabinet door. "Because I did. You seemed so confident. I wanted to be like you."

"You're better than me." He leaned forward and put his face in her periphery. "You're a *legend*."

He was teasing her. She looked at him, a slice of anger interrupting her renewed admiration of him. She knew who she was. She had talents, gifts. She was so sick of people underestimating her, thinking because she came from a semi-crazy family she wasn't capable.

She slammed her cup down and hot tea splashed across her hand. 'Ow. Dammit."

He immediately grabbed her hand and led her to the sink. He turned on the water and held her hand under it.

Wow, he had large hands and a few more callouses than she'd think an attorney would have.

The water felt great, his hands even better. Warm, strong. "Okay?"

"What? Oh, yes. Thanks." She withdrew her hand in case her annoying lusty feelings toward the man replaced her sliver of anger. Being a little miffed at him under the surface was good. It kept her mind thinking straight around him for once.

His eyes softened. "I am sorry. I don't know why I said any of those things. I shouldn't have. I'm…" He scrubbed his hair. "Sorry."

Wow. He seemed to be for real. Second time tonight, too.

She looked up at him. "I tried to kiss you." There. Bloody band-aid ripped off. And, *guh*, it was humiliating. She must have resembled the Pantone spectrum of reds right then. But he should know the whole story so they could put it behind them.

He laughed. Actually *chuckled*. Then he arched an eyebrow. "How would I get so lucky?"

"You said you'd never kiss a Bloom." Wait… lucky?

His face stilled. The dragon fire she'd seen before in his

eyes? Totally back. "I don't remember knowing anything about your family."

"We were the crazy family with the ostriches and truffle pigs." Her voice was flat like she was reciting a recipe for something.

But then something dawned in his fiery eyes. The heat then cooled as quickly as it arose, maybe replaced by remorse. "Ooooh."

"See? It's all coming back now."

"Some. Not the part where I blew it, though. I must have blanked it from my mind. Not getting to…"

He stopped abruptly. He glanced down at her mouth.

"To what?" She rolled her lips between her teeth.

He reached over, his large hand cupping her cheek. He thumb pulled on her lip so she released them, then dropped his hand. "I shouldn't have done that."

"You can totally do that." She hugged the back of her arms and spun away. Her mouth, always a maverick, was operating on its own. It was his eyes again. He should have been a hypnotist.

His hands on her shoulders turned her back toward him. And then he was bending over, his lips so close to hers she could barely see him anymore. "Can I make it right?"

She swallowed and nodded.

His lips then met hers.

Fourteen years she'd wondered, dreamed, imagined what this moment might be like. She'd been wrong about it all. Her mind couldn't have understood what was possible.

Strong lips slid over hers. One arm circled the small of her back and brought her flush to him while the other wrapped around her neck. No dithering. No fumbling. Just full-on mouth assault. She was such willing prey.

Her entire body wilted in his hold, and that only made his

arms, his hands, his mouth take more. Two magnets couldn't have gotten closer.

And her body was *so* on board. Take her. Use her. Do anything, it screamed. Wring her out and hang her up to dry because nothing—*nothing*—was staying dry in this position.

Sweet Jesus on high, this man was…

He broke the kiss and stepped backward. "I shouldn't have."

She sucked in air and quickly swallowed. "Yes, you should, and if you'd done that before—"

"You were fourteen. I did the right thing then, not kissing you."

She nodded. "You do like your rules." Even if he was right about that one. So, the arrogant bastard had some standards albeit meted out harshly. She'd always been raised to go for it and ask for forgiveness later. But look what trouble that had gotten her into her entire freaking life.

Whatever, let the mayhem continue. She stepped forward, and he took a step back.

He raised his chin. "The man you choose is going to be one lucky bastard."

Could he appear to regret kissing her anymore? She took a second to center herself before answering. "Yes, he is. And you'll go out with Sally." She nodded as if convincing herself.

"There's nothing wrong with me attending a local function with a member of the academy board. It's good for Maribelle." His bossy voice was back.

She didn't get that logic at all, but God knew what went on in Ashton's Scott's mind. They were two magnets alright, now facing the wrong way, repelling one another.

She didn't need tea. She certainly didn't need more Ashton Scott kisses. They were lethal. And they'd done their job. She would compare every man to him forever. Just like Maribelle. Because that's what Ashton Scott did. He made indelible impressions. He won on any field he played on. Every time.

She got out of there as fast she could. She jogged through the house, up the stairs, and back to her bed with its 1000 count, imported Egyptian cotton, and she had no idea what to do next.

Carry on as if he hadn't kissed her and let her hang to dry?

Quit?

Stay?

She didn't have time to decide because a little cry broke into her thoughts. Maribelle. Next door. She flew to her room and found the little girl crying, scrambling back to the headboard.

As Addy consoled her, her decision was clear. She couldn't leave this little girl. She didn't know how she could stay in a house with a man she couldn't stop thinking about —thoughts that would shock a porn star. But she would. She'd work for a man who dangled himself in front of her and then promptly rejected her—again.

16

Ash didn't lie to himself. He was an asshole as a teen. So were his friends. It's how they survived boarding school. One-upping one another. Slamming each other. Old habits were hard, weren't they?

Clearly, because he'd done it again to Adelaide who, quite frankly, didn't deserve it. She may be annoyance central, but he had no right to kiss her.

She had to look at him with her sad, blue-gray eyes, and twist her pretty pink lips, and tell him something awful about himself. He'd wanted to make it right somehow.

Kissing her was a new experience. None of that smeary lipstick crap women were so fond of wearing. Just warm, natural lips that fit so well against his.

Now, he had to avoid her at all costs. Work helped.

He stared down at the brief he was supposed to be finishing. He slunk back into his office chair, a perfect fit—usually. Rose. Began to pace. Paused at the large window overlooking the backyard. The landscapers were cutting the bushes. His ears strained to hear Adelaide and Maribelle upstairs. Nothing.

It'd been a few days since he'd spent more than five minutes in the room with them during the day. But at night? Avoiding his nanny wasn't so easy. Maribelle cried out with nightmares more often now for some reason. He couldn't beat Adelaide to Maribelle's bedside. And Lord knew he tried. He'd shoo her away at the door, but one look at Adelaide and Maribelle would stop crying. So, she had to stay. He supposed he could let Adelaide handle it.

No. He couldn't let one nanny get between them. A nanny he was growing increasingly obsessed with understanding—like how she handled Maribelle so well. Like how she could still even look at him and not want to punch his lights out after he'd been such a bastard to her twice now.

It was that damn kiss. It took a supreme effort to not glance at her lips every night as they'd help Maribelle fall back asleep. It was even harder when they both backed out of the room to go back to the respective corners. Neither one broached the subject of that night in the kitchen. Rather, they'd turn away and head back to their rooms.

He'd ease himself back into his bed and spend an hour thinking about Adelaide in hers. Her dark hair fanned out on a pillowcase. Her eyes blinking up at the ceiling.

Who was he kidding? She probably nodded off right away. He, however, who *had* been sleeping like the dead, now tossed and turned most nights, trying to ignore the increasing hardness between his legs.

He cracked his knuckles, a habit he'd broken years ago. He should be in a far greater mood than he'd been of late. The Transom deal finally came in. The headlines had quieted. Maribelle would start school soon. He'd then have choices for the first time in over a year, like leaving this godforsaken place.

He scrubbed his chin, his gaze going soft over the huge expanse of green. He'd spent most of his time back there as a kid—hell, the few times he was allowed to *be* a kid in this place.

The sound of a motor gearing up cut into his thoughts. The worst sound on the planet roared into the air.

A leafblower.

He trudged toward the sound to talk to the landscapers. His brief wouldn't complete itself, and if his own mind wouldn't give him some peace, at least his own house should.

His feet hit the parquet floor of the entryway and the loud trill of a piano run joined the infernal noise. Then, the thumping of feet. The girls were having another dance party, no doubt.

Once he made his way to the back door, he signaled the guy with the blasted machine over.

He idled it and ambled over.

"Hey, can you come back tomorrow?"

The man wiped his brow. "Not sure I can. Got a schedule to keep."

"Skip it. Consider the job done."

The guy shrugged, turned off the machine together—blessed peace filling the air—and strode away.

For long minutes, he stood there, the late summer breeze running over his face. The backyard used to be a riot of hydrangeas, azaleas, and silly garden gnome statues. Funny, he hadn't thought of that in ages. The place was a bit run-down now.

He spun to head back into the house when Maribelle launched herself at him. "Daddy, Daddy, you're going to build my tree castle now, right?"

"I believe your father has work to do."

He straightened to find Adelaide standing in the open French door. Sunlight lit up her face.

"I could take a minute to assess the structure." His five-mile run that morning hadn't done a thing to calm down the urge to move.

Adelaide snickered. "Yes, the structure should be assessed."

"Don't believe in structure?"

She crossed her arms. "I'm surprised you would have time."

He held out his hand to Maribelle, who took it. "Why don't you show me where you want it?"

She pointed toward the old oak tree. "Right there. Then I can assess my kingdom."

He chuckled and glanced up at his defiant nanny. "Yes, assessing is a good thing to do."

A smirk formed on her face, but she lazily took the step down to the terrace and traipsed over. Maribelle reached out and took her hand so they both had a hold of her.

The three of them made their way to the tree in the dead center of the yard. He peered up at the old boards barely hanging on in the crook of three large branches. "That's seen better days."

"I know a guy who can handle that." Adelaide craned her neck up, revealing a long expanse of tan skin.

"I'm sure you do."

Her chin dropped and her mouth dropped open. *Jesus*, she brought the snark out in him.

He scrubbed his head. "I didn't mean it like that."

"I'm sure you didn't." She added a level of cheer to her voice as if to say nothing he did was going to bother her.

Something buzzed by his head, and he swatted at it. "I can build it. No need to hire anyone."

She arched an eyebrow. She didn't think he could, did she? Maribelle, however, jumped up and down, displaying a heart-warming belief in him. "Paint it yellow."

"Excellent color choice, Queen Maribelle." Addy nodded

her head. "And I'm sure your father will build an excellent castle."

She stared at him. Her eyes softened toward him. Was she relaying a truce? He hoped like hell so. Maybe the time apart had been the right choice instead of jumping into explanations, apologies…

Another infernal buzzing flew by his ear. Then it seemed to circle his head. He swatted at it anew. "The ladder, too?"

"All of it, Daddy."

"Hey, Maribelle, mind running inside and asking Miss Stevens for a tape measure?"

She squealed and was off like a shot.

Adelaide cocked her head. "Getting started so soon?"

"Why not? Plus, I wanted a second with you. To apologize for the other night." He swatted at the bug that seemed to be in love with him.

She chewed on her bottom lip which only made the memory of tasting them flood back to his senses. His mouth watered.

She shook her head. "It's okay. Forget it. It was—"

"Don't say 'nothing.'" He waved his hand once more at the droning that would not quit.

"I wasn't. I was going to say a mistake."

Was it? "I was out of line."

Her eyes grew wide. "Don't move."

Greater buzzing began and then his neck burst with pain. He slapped at it. *Goddammit.* His hand drew away pieces of bug. Two more of the wretched devils were running circles around him.

"Hornets," she called. A pounding of feet on grass came next. Adelaide was fleeing the scene.

He, however, proceeded to dance like a ninja on steroids, trying to get away from the accursed things that were locked in on him like two jet fighters.

The house was at least thirty feet away, and as he moved toward it, the things followed him. Another sharp sting on his arm—through his shirt, of all things—made his arm explode in fire.

His feet hit the first of the stone steps leading up to the terrace just as a stream of water worthy of dousing a house-fire hit him square in the face. He swatted his hands in front of it. Every curse word known to man flew out of his mouth.

Adelaide's voice cut through his screaming. "Stop moving! I almost got them."

She was trying to drown him. He pushed forward and broke through the accursed stream of water and yelled. "Stop. Right. Now."

The water mercifully stopped attacking him. He spluttered and his gaze found her and Maribelle. They stood by the water spigot, the garden hose limping from Adelaide's hand.

"Water. Gets them every time." She cranked the faucet off and radiated a smile at him.

He let out a cough. He was doused from head to toe. His shirt stuck to him. Even his pants were glued to his thighs. He pulled out his phone from his front pants pocket. A long drip, drip, drip fell from it.

The only good thing about his situation was that ferocious buzzing around his body had stopped. It was now replaced with the sound of water drops hitting the stones under his feet.

Movement in his periphery caught his eye. Two figures stood in the open French doors. Stevens and Sally Albrecchio.

For a long second, they stood staring at one another, listening to the sound of water dribbling off the edge of the terrace.

"My." Sally was the first to break the silence and step onto the wet stones. "We are into watersports, aren't we?"

Her head slowly swiveled to face Adelaide. They glared at one another. Adelaide was the first to break the contact and turn back to him. "At least this time it wasn't filmed."

That's when he realized today was Wednesday. He hadn't shown up at the art gallery reception the previous night to meet Sally. It'd completely slipped his mind.

17

Adelaide gingerly stepped up the stairs, peering around the tray she held. Cutlery clanged against the plate on the tray and a little water splashed over the goblet to darken the placemat under the setting. She and Maribelle were going to play "room service." It was one of Maribelle's requests tonight. The fact that a little girl knew what room service was at her age was ridiculous. Addy supposed she'd had her share of eating it.

But, whatever she wanted, Addy was fine to deliver.

Maribelle had had a crying jag that afternoon because she overheard Ash and Sally talking—mostly *whispering*—about dinner. As in, *going out to dinner.* You never know what's going to "ignite" a six-year-old little girl. She just hadn't realized how much hearing Ash was being a total fool when it came to Sally would do the same to her.

Just when she thought she wasn't angry at him anymore... Adelaide may never get over the sight of Sally's smug face as she glanced over to her when Ash had said, "Why don't you meet me back here? Give me a chance to get cleaned up and get Maribelle settled. We'll go together from here."

Victory spread over her face like a stain. The thought of Sally putting her hands on him, kissing him… Addy shuddered, making the knife and fork on the tray clink again.

If only he hadn't kissed her. She could have gone her whole life without knowing how good he was with his mouth. Now he ticked every sense. He looked good. He smelled good. He touched well. Now she knew he tasted incredibly good—like warm tea and honey.

The hallway was particularly still as she rose to the second floor. Downstairs, in the distance, Miss Stevens' voice murmured. Probably on the phone. The woman never stopped working, usually sequestered in the little room off the library she called her office.

She was better at hiding than Addy was, though she'd done a spectacular job avoiding Ash for the last few days, at least until this afternoon. Or perhaps he had done a stellar job of avoiding *her*. Either way, she thought they'd finally got through their after-kiss awkwardness thanks to a little distance. They'd talked about it. It was over.

Addy turned the corner and stopped a few feet from Maribelle's bedroom door.

Ash and Maribelle were having "tea." He sat in profile across from Maribelle. They had similar noses. In other words, perfect.

Whoever said men looking all tough was the hottest thing ever never saw Ashton Scott sitting at a tiny table in a chair that barely fit one of his butt cheeks holding a tiny yellow cup with daisies on it. The New York publishing scene could develop and sell a whole calendar with just pictures of Ashton Scott doing different things with his daughter.

"And what kind of tea are we drinking, Maribelle?" He

held it up to his lips and smiled. He should smile more often. It was good—all those white teeth in a tanned face rocking that shadowy beard across his jawline.

Maribelle smoothed down her skirt. "Magic marshmallow tea. It was mommy's favorite."

"It's magic, huh?"

She nodded once and snuffed up the last of her tears. "Yes."

Lines around his eyes softened.

Addy leaned against the door frame, getting all inappropriately swoony. But what else could she expect from herself? She was a grown woman, and Ashton Scott was aphrodisiac central.

"Here." He reached over and pulled her little chair around. "Want me to do your hair?"

She blinked up at him, only having eyes for him. "Yes, please." Oh, man, she truly would compare every man to her father. Then again, so would Addy.

Maribelle twisted and presented her back to him. She pulled one of her dolls into her lap.

He slipped off his watch and then wrapped two large strands of her dark hair through his thick fingers. He twisted and plaited her long locks into a braid. Ah, braiding penance for all the earlier yelling—which had included some curse words Addy had never heard before. Hornets could bring out the devil in a priest.

Ash pressed a kiss to the back of her head, and Addy took in a stuttered breath.

Oh, my God. There was a new level of hotness that he could reach. Total big daddy energy.

Maribelle's arm flapped. "Addy! Addy! Have some tea."

Ash's face dropped upon seeing her. Okay, compassion vanished. Freezy face in its place. It was as if he purposefully erased all emotion from his features at seeing her.

It was for the best.

Addy pushed off the door frame and held up her tray. "Ready for room service?"

"When Daddy finishes doing my hair."

She'd certainly learned how to wrap him around her fingers—all ten of them. Addy couldn't help but smile, and amazingly, Ash returned one to her.

Holding a braid in one hand, he used his other to move tiny plastic cups and saucers.

She set the tray down. "You know how to French braid." Could this man do everything well?

"Old girlfriends."

Why, yes, he could, including doing a fine job of stabbing her through the heart with his admission. Not "girlfriend" but plural "girlfriends."

She had to get a handle on her reactions to him and his romantic status, past or present. He wasn't hers to get jealous over.

So what if he'd rejected her and then moved on to girlfriends who knew how to French braid?

Maribelle's eyes drooped a little.

"Queen Maribelle, you feeling okay?"

"I'm fine. Thank you for asking."

"Mr. Scott." Miss Stevens materialized in the doorway. "Ms. Albrecchio is here."

"I'll be right down."

She nodded once and sliced her eyes toward Addy. A slight tightening of her lips was all Addy needed to understand how Stevens felt about this little scene. This is what life with him was like, wasn't it? Everyone around him feeling they should be his partner, not anyone else.

He twisted the final locks of Maribelle's hair. "There you go, my little Belle."

Addy pulled a hair band from her wrist and handed it to him to use.

Maribelle skipped over to her full-length mirror and checked her braids.

"She's her mother's daughter alright." Ash's voice held a new tone. Wistful, perhaps? He rose and peered down at her. "Have everything you need for tonight?"

She nodded, not knowing what to say. "Is this another time I should say I'm sorry? I mean, for…" She waved her hand toward the back of the house.

"For saving me from a hornet's wrath?" He shook his head.

"Well, you cleaned up well."

He gazed down at his shiny shoes, his neatly pressed trousers, his crisp button-down, and sharp suitcoat. He lifted his lashes. "Maybe I should ask Maribelle if she approves?"

They both glanced over at Maribelle, who was sitting cross-legged and practicing "faces" in the mirrors—likely another activity she'd gotten from her mother.

"Something tells me she'd have told you by now."

He chuckled at that. "I won't be late." He headed to the doorway. "Night, Maribelle."

She frowned at him in the mirror. "Tuck me in when you get back."

"Addy is going to do it."

Maribelle huffed and set her chin on her hands.

"Oh, you'll be out that late, huh?" If Sally had anything to do with it, she'd keep him all night through breakfast.

"Past 7:30 at least? Yes." He dripped his chin and adopted a mock-serious face. "And you'll make sure…"

"To get her to bed on time." She crossed her heart and held up two fingers. "I promise. It's the one rule I'm pretty good at."

He winked at her. "Goodnight, Addy."

He strode out, and if the minuscule air currents his large frame produced could create a wake, they would have toppled her over.

He'd called her Addy.

18

—————

After drying off, changing clothes, and getting Maribelle settled, Ash jogged down the wide staircase to the foyer. Stevens and Sally's voices drifted from the library. He found them chatting amicably on the couch before the fireplace, each holding a glass of wine.

They'd chummed up quickly.

He cleared his throat. "Ms. Albrecchio, sorry for the delay."

Both women rose at seeing him. "Sally, please, and no problem. I've been having a lovely chat with Miss Stevens here."

His assistant gave him a look he recognized. She wasn't fooled by Sally and had likely fielded the barrage of questions as he would have: with as little information as possible.

"We won't be late," he said to her.

"I'm calling it a night." She nodded once and scooted out, still holding her wine. Perhaps now the woman would actually take the night off. She rarely did.

Sally stepped up to him and lifted her glass. "You have good taste."

"I try." He glanced at the lip print she'd left on the rim and held back a shudder. He could do this, make up for standing her up last night. It was just one night. Two drinks. A dinner at some local joint that he'd let Sally choose.

He held out his arm. "Shall we?"

She set her glass down on the console table near the door and took his offer.

"I appreciate the opportunity to make last night up to you," he said.

She waved her hand. "These things happen. And Adelaide does have a way of distracting people."

"I got swamped with work."

"Well, whatever the reason, this is probably better. Then we can really talk. Not get distracted. I can fill you in on anything you might need to know." Her eyes sliced to the stairway.

Adelaide was pounding down them. She held up his watch with one finger. "You forgot this. I wouldn't want you to lose track of time."

She was nearly breathless as she skidded to a stop before them.

"Thank you." He took the watch from her and slipped it onto his wrist, clicking it into place.

Sally's eyes widened. Great, something else he was going to have to explain.

He shook his wrist a little. "I was braiding Maribelle's hair. It gets caught."

Sally let out a long, drawn-out, "Oh." Her smile returned. "It's nice to see someone who's hands-on with their children."

"Mr. Scott is a wonderful father," Adelaide interjected quickly. "He does a lot of things with Maribelle. In fact, I'd say he does more with his daughter than most fathers I've seen."

His insides swelled with surprise and his feet might have lifted off the ground for a second. Her words were laced with a sincerity he hadn't expected. He'd heard enough of them in his day to know when someone was telling the truth or not. She believed her words.

Adelaide spun on her heel and vanished back up the staircase. He hadn't realized he'd been staring at her until Sally put herself in his view.

"I must admit I was surprised to see Adelaide was still your nanny. Isn't she a temp?"

"She's permanent." That word rolled right out of his mouth. He couldn't imagine her not being around.

"I see." She lifted both eyebrows and nodded.

"What?"

"It's just…people are talking."

"Oh, the pictures, the water balloons. Like Miss Bloom said, I do a lot of things with my daughter."

"And your nanny. But I'm sure Addy goaded you into that."

"Not really." He shouldn't be continuing this line of conversation, but he didn't like the way she said Adelaide's name. It was as if she couldn't wait to spit it out, like sour milk.

Sally sighed. "She has ideas that you're going to want to watch. There are rumors of… I shouldn't gossip."

She wanted to gossip—badly. Another thing he was well-versed in when it came to the human race.

He gestured to the front door. "Let's go, shall we?"

Her heels clicked on his front walkway as they walked side by side toward his car. He hoped he didn't regret this dinner because he had a feeling he was going to be deflecting not only questions but small-town dirt.

Truth was, he did want to know more about Adelaide. He just didn't want to hear it from Sally. He wanted to hear it from Adelaide herself. Learning about her any other way moved into a disloyal territory he wouldn't visit.

Strange. Normally, he'd use any means to find out about a person. Hell, he'd done it his whole life as an attorney. Ferreting out every weakness of the opposition, every piece of information about colleagues to ensure he could trust them was merely good business.

Something had shifted between him and Adelaide, however. *Hell, ya' think, Scott?* He'd kissed her. They'd fought. They'd made up—sort of. He didn't know where they stood. And he'd figure it out, just not through anyone's perceptions but his own.

Sally had chosen a small Italian place attached to an inn on the other side of town. She chatted away, pointing out various Moorsville landmarks along the way. At least the woman waited until they were seated at a small table in the corner before she began to hint she knew things about Adelaide.

He then spent the greater part of the evening, over a meal of eggplant parmesan, red wine, and tiramisu, deflecting any talk of his nanny.

So, how's it going? With Maribelle?
Wonderfully.
And you have all the help you need?
Yes.
Because if you need a more seasoned nanny—
I don't.
Then you might want to know—
I don't.

She'd smile and wait at least another fifteen minutes before again attempting to discuss Maribelle's caregiver, all under the guise of preparing his daughter for school.

It was the longest dinner of his life.

19

Ash swung his car around in his circular drive, his headlights lighting up the back of a Daisy's Deliveries van. A figure darted around the back of it and screamed.

It was Scarlett, Adelaide's sister. "Jesus. Warn a girl, will ya'?"

He cracked open the door and shouted into the night. "It's my house." He rose and slammed his car door shut. "Delivering daisies?"

She folded her arms over her chest and cocked a hip. She was most definitely related to Adelaide.

"Wool socks and honey from our family farm."

"Oh?" He peered up at the windows of Maribelle's room. A low glow emanated. He didn't recall her night-light glowing so brightly.

"Yes, and don't worry. Maribelle is going to be fine. Addy is great at this. Legendary."

His gaze shot to her face and his feet carried him closer to her. "What do you mean? What's wrong with Maribelle?" Without waiting for an answer, he spun and was up the steps and into the house, leaving Scarlett sputtering something in the background.

Inside the entryway, he skidded to a stop. Adelaide was coming down the stairs holding a bucket. Her eyes flew wide, and she half-crouched toward the banister. "Jesus. Warn a girl."

"It's. My. House."

She visibly swallowed at his bark.

He strode forward. "What's wrong with Maribelle?" An image of Maribelle's pale face rose up in his mind. The fear as she clutched her doll while she crouched in the corner of her closet. That strange woman who'd broken into their New York apartment smiling down at her.

Adelaide pursed her lips. "Nothing big. Just a smidge of a temperature." She lifted up the bucket.

"What's that?"

"Cold water. Sock treatment. Works every time. The twenty-four-hour pharmacy already sent everything over. Pedialyte, ginger ale. But they didn't have children's wool socks, so that's why Scarlett came by. Hey, you got any lemons?"

Socks? Lemons? Had the woman lost her mind? He pulled out his phone. "We need a doctor." He stared down at the screen. The thing was useless. He didn't know any doctors in town. "Who do you know?" He looked up at her and her forehead wrinkled.

She gave him the side-eye. "Know?"

"A doctor." He said the word slowly as if talking to an imbecile. His nerves were beyond frayed thanks to spending two hours with a woman whose hand could not stay on her side of the table. It kept drifting to his wrist, his arm.

Adelaide joined him down on the landing. "She doesn't need one. A little lemon-honey tea and the socks will do it." She drew even closer to him.

"Hardly."

"Look, her temp is nothing. It's—"

"Don't say it's nothing." His jaw was going to shatter.

Adelaide's finger flew to her lips. "Shhhh."

Scolded in his own house? "Excuse me?"

"You'll wake her up."

Fat chance given they were so far away. He took the steps to the second floor two at a time. He tried hard to ignore the huff coming from Adelaide behind him.

There are seven types of over-protective parents—tiger, helicopter, hothouse, best friend, trust fund, bulldozer, and head-in-the-sand parenting styles.

Ash was most definitely a bulldozer.

Addy set down the bucket and jogged after him, sure he'd bluster in and wake her up. She hadn't read *The Princesses Shoes* four times for nothing.

She could barely keep up with him. In fact, he lost her halfway up the stairway. She should have known Ash would lose his ever-loving mind when he learned Maribelle was sick.

Maybe Maribelle's condition would distract him from whatever Sally had told him at dinner because, for sure, that woman did not miss a golden chance to tell him everything. All night she'd worked all the stories Sally likely told him over and over in her mind.

Adelaide is trouble. She's a heartbreaker. She's one for revenge.

The minute Ash was out the door, Maribelle flopped into bed whimpering about her body *betraying* her—her exact words.

Addy couldn't find miss Stevens anywhere. She couldn't leave to get the necessary socks. So, she called for reinforcements, namely Scarlett, who had a date but managed to swing by with socks and a wholly inadequate, "Don't worry about Ash. Maybe he'll think what we did to Bryson was funny," platitude when Scarlett gushed out the news about his date and the likelihood Sally spilled everything.

Funny, huh? Ash would probably change the locks on his house after Sally got through with him.

When she got to Maribelle's room, the little girl was awake, her eyes at half-mast, her little fingers working the dress on her doll that she clutched.

Ash knelt by her bedside as his hand brushed the hair off her forehead. "Can I get you anything? Some ginger ale? Or… tea?"

Maribelle drew in a stuttered breath and sent her glassy eyes up to him. "No, I don't feel good."

"I know, baby." Man, his little girl learned how to eke out the most sympathy from her father—fast.

"But Addy gave me the socks." She pushed her covers down and pulled out her leg. "See?"

Adelaide drew closer to them. "Yes, the special, magic, yellow ones."

His lips drew a sour line at seeing the thin, yellow cotton socks over the thicker, gray wool pair. "I see."

He drew up the covers to her chin again. "Why don't you go to sleep? I'll sit with you for a while."

She turned on her side and clutched the sheet under her chin. "Miss Charlotte is going to watch over us tonight."

He chewed the inside of his cheek as her eyes drifted close. It didn't take long for her to start making little kitten snores.

Ash stood and adjusted her covers, picked up a doll on the floor, and nestled it against her. He then reached over, grabbed the bottle of Pedialyte, and began to read the label, studying it hard. So hard, in fact, he might have burst some capillaries in his eyes. Addy was afraid to interrupt him.

The Exalted One was completely undone. It was adorable, endearing, and mind-boggling. Kids got sick all the time, like it was their job.

He glanced over at Adelaide. "Let's talk outside."

Like a puppy, she followed him to the hallway.

He sighed and scrubbed his hand down his face. "Was she throwing up?" He lifted the bottle.

"No, but that replenishes the electrolytes so I thought it couldn't hurt. Has she never been sick before?"

He shook his head. "Not with me."

"Well, it's good for their immunity. They need to get sick every once in a while to build up those antibodies. And it's just a hundred fever. Not as high as I've seen, if that makes you feel any better."

One of his eyebrows crooked upward. "Nothing about this is going to make me feel better."

She stepped closer to him and touched his arm in an attempt to provide some friendly comfort. He nearly plastered himself against the wall as if she'd tried to brand him or something.

She jumped backward. "Sorry." Could the man act any more disgusted? Dammit, Sally had told him everything, hadn't she?

His forehead wrinkled. "Where's Stevens? I need her to find me a pediatrician."

Oh, maybe Sally didn't spill it all? Or his memory was terrible? "She left hours ago. But I can tell you who would be best. He won't get into the office until nine tomorrow. Dr. Morgansten."

"Okay. I'll call in the morning. Listen, the socks? I can appreciate this whole magic thing to make her feel better, but—"

"It's actually not magic."

"Glad to hear you say that."

"But it works like a charm. Didn't your mom ever do the sock treatment on you? It's been around forever."

He huffed in answer. "My mother wasn't exactly the sit-up-all-night kind of mom. We'll see what a doctor says."

His mom had been kind to her, but clearly, he didn't have the same experience. It was none of Addy's business. Maribelle was. "This is how it works: the body will work hard to keep her feet warm, and it kicks the immune system into high gear."

He harumphed. Okay, he still was not a fan of her techniques. He stared down at the carpeting. "I shouldn't have left tonight." He sucked in a long breath. "Listen, you go ahead and go to bed. I got this."

Ash returned to Maribelle's room and settled on his butt on the large butterfly carpet by her bed, his arms circling his knees. He was going to spend all night here, wasn't he? He stared at Maribelle like he was afraid to take his eyes off her.

Yeah, now was not the time for her own self-preservation, like drilling him on exactly what Sally had spilled. If he fired her in the morning, so be it. For now, taking care of Maribelle was a priority.

She should go sit with him. It felt wrong to leave them like this.

Maybe she'd make him some tea. She hustled to the kitchen. It took her no time at all to boil some water and start steeping two cups of chamomile. She tipped a teaspoon of whiskey she found in a cupboard containing a number of liquor bottles into one of them. *What the hell.*

When she returned to Maribelle's room, he'd stretched out his legs, his back against the nightstand. His legs ran down the center of the large butterfly carpet, making it look like he'd sprouted wings.

The poor guys who fell for Maribelle in about ten years were in so much trouble. They'd have to lasso the star system to compete with the attention Ash gave his daughter.

He was a parenting style all his own. Hovercraft. That's what she'd label him.

Addy settled herself across from Ash and lifted both cups of tea toward him. "The one with whiskey or the one without?" she whispered.

Her question got a half-smile out of him.

She handed him the one with the liquor. He took a sip, and the creases around his mouth deepened as if he fought a smile. "You do like your holistic methods." The rasp of his tone sent a tingle down her spine.

"They work," she mouthed over the rim of her cup.

"Like the magic socks?" He took another sip.

"Like the works-every-time socks. You do know she's going to fine, right? I promise. In fact, her little immune system is kicking ass right now. She will be stronger tomorrow because of this. It's how kids work."

He scrubbed his fingers against his growing beard. His incredibly sexy beard, if she noticed. She was trying so hard not to notice.

He stared into his cup. "It's times like this that…"

"What?"

"I wish her mother was here."

She could understand that. "But you're here."

He nodded slowly.

She didn't know what might make this man feel better. Maybe stay silent for once? Plus, she was worried if she opened her mouth again, a barrage of questions about his date would tumble out. That was the last thing this man needed. So, they sat for long minutes in a strained silence.

The grandfather clock downstairs chimed softly. The drone of insects out the window grew louder. And Addy tried hard not to stare at Ash, whose eyes remained fixed on Maribelle. Only Ash Scott could look even more masculine sitting on a child's butterfly rug.

Every once in a while, he'd send his gaze her way and she'd have to rip her eyes to something—anything—else in the room. His eyes sent a familiar rush of warmth through her whole body. Sometimes when he looked at her, she imagined he could see into her mind and sense the dreams she'd had about him.

Not even fatigue like heavy wet blankets on her could stop her mind from *going there.* It was because his scent, his heat, his whole freaking body was too close to hers. Her belly danced with the thought he'd mindread all the filthy, carnal things that spiraled through her thoughts when she slept.

Finally, Adelaide couldn't hold her head up any longer and she rested it on the bed. Their knees were so close, they nearly touched. His nearby heat was oddly comforting.

She didn't know how long they stayed like that because she began to drift. It wasn't until a bright light cut through the haze that she woke. Her lids were sticky and she came face to face with a bright pink elephant plushie.

20

Jesus, it was hot. Like she'd fallen asleep on a scorching furnace.

She tried to sit up, but a large arm held her close.

Her eyes snapped open.

Holy Hades. Her leg was draped over Ash's thigh, her head on his bicep, and his chest rose and fell under her arm. They were tangled up in each other on the floor.

She should ease herself out. She just couldn't make herself. He felt too good. Maybe she could take a minute... There was nothing like waking up with the smell of a man so close. All that hardness under your limbs.

No. *Get out,* screamed her logical self.

She tried to move, but his arm tightened. This could not be happening. He was actually holding her. There went Addy's panties—for the hundredth time.

Oh, man. Please, don't let her have snored. Please, please, please.

Ash's diaphram kicked in and he sucked in a long breath. His hold released and he eased his arm out. Adelaide scooted backward to separate herself from him.

At seeing her, his eyes rounded like twin moons. "Oh, excuse me."

The man adopted formality so fast. She shrugged. "Spontaneous sleepover?"

He cleared his throat and glanced over at Maribelle. There was good color in her cheeks and she was sleeping soundly.

His hand reached out to her forehead. "Huh," he said. "Feels normal." He ran his hand down his mouth and chin.

Maribelle stirred and blinked up at him. "Hi, Daddy." She then rolled over and faced the wall, clutching her doll and fell promptly back to sleep.

The amount of relief coursing off his body lightened the air in the room. He shook his head slowly, a half-smile inching up on his face. "I'd give anything to sleep as well as that."

Wouldn't we all? She stretched her neck, which she would likely have a crick in all day. So worth it, though.

She jumped to standing. "Be right back." She nearly ran to Maribelle's bathroom except she was so stiff she likely resembled a seal on dry land, but she had to pee like a race-horse so she had no choice. She also wanted to wash out her mouth because morning breath.

When she came out, he was still sitting by Maribelle's bed, swigging water from a bottle she'd left there last night.

"Want some coffee?" She tried to sound casual, breezy.

He yawned and pushed himself to standing. "I'll go with you. Need to stretch my legs."

She headed to the door and promptly bumped into him. He caught her before she sprawled at his feet. "Oh, sorry. Morning feet." With no sense of direction or balance, maybe it was because her neck was kinked up and stopped the blood flow to her brain and limbs.

He gestured for her to walk through the doorway first,

probably to make sure he didn't get any more bruised. Was she always this klutzy after falling asleep tangled up with her hot boss? How would she know? She'd never done it before. What was the protocol for doing the most awkward thing one can do?

Ignore it happened at all, like their kitchen kiss. That's what she could do.

But then she spun to face him, and he was so close, her hands shot up and landed on his pecs. He closed one hand over hers and stared down at her. He was looking at her lips.

"Thanks for being here last night. Talking me off the ledge." He cocked his head. "I'm still… figuring it all out."

"You are. Like I said, you're a good father." She swallowed.

"You're a good nanny." He dropped his hand and brushed a hair off her cheek.

It was so intimate, she froze.

"You look surprised. Don't believe me?" he asked.

"I thought for sure Sally would have turned you off forever on me." Oh, man, that just came out. "Listen…" A quick glance at Maribelle showed a marching band might parade through the room and she wasn't waking up anytime soon. "About your date last night and what she might have—"

"It wasn't a date," he said rather forcefully.

Why did that make her feel so much better? Even if she did paint Adelaide as the devil's concubine, the last thing she'd want is for Ash to get tangled in Sally's super web. Black widows were friendlier. "Does Sally know that?"

He dropped his hand. "I doubt it. You're probably right about her. But it doesn't matter." Ash cleared his throat. "And about my *meeting* with her. It's clear—"

"Is this the part where you say I'm not a good fit? You'll give me a good reference?"

His eyebrows pinched together. "No. Why would you ask—"

"I'm sure she told you things about me."

"She seemed quite interested—"

"Oh, I'm sure."

"Adelaide." His blue eyes flamed.

Okay, she was fully awake now thanks to his whispered bellow.

He cleared his throat as if about to deliver some important information. Here it came, right?

"She appeared quite interested in my relationship with you, but," he held up his finger when she moved to speak, "it's none of her business."

"Relationship." Addy leaned back, cushioning her tailbone with her hands against the door jamb. "Yeah, she doesn't like that I have one with you at all. Or any man."

"She's probably bought into all the clichés. Boss. Hot nanny." He was trying to be funny, lighten things up, wasn't he?

"Hot nanny?" A little snort came out of her nose. "Now you're just being polite."

"I'm not that polite." He drew in a breath. "Clearly. Which brings me to our kiss in the kitchen. We never cleared things up there."

She pushed off from her lean, and he held up his hands. "Again, I apologize. I won't kiss you again if that's what you're worried about."

"I'm not worried. It was a good kiss."

"It was?" He sounded surprised. My God, it was the best kiss she'd ever had.

"Want a number?" She mock-punched him. "I mean, my sister would totally rate you. Tell you that you're…"

He closed the distance between them. "What?"

She had to lift her chin to look up at his face. His blue eyes were locked on her lips, which made her heartbeat race —like NASCAR level speed. "She'd say a fifteen."

"Out of?" He arched an eyebrow.

That made her smile. Ash Scott was concerned about his abilities? Or he was humoring her? "Ten."

One side of his mouth lifted into a half-smile. "Then yes. Kissing you was most definitely a fifteen." He inched even closer to her, so close the heat of his body warmed her skin. "And to be honest, I'm not sorry."

Forget her heartbeat, prickles drew up her spine, her neck, her cheeks so fast she nearly shuddered. "Neither am I. You can. Again."

He waited a long second and stared at her. Then he pressed her against the door frame and kissed her. It was even better than before.

21

───────

He inhaled Adelaide's slight floral scent and moved his mouth over her impossibly soft lips.

She just had to look at him with those eager eyes. Suddenly, it'd been a little hard to breathe. He'd lost all sense of himself when her throat bobbed in a delicate swallow, and all he could think of was pressing his lips there, that little dip above her breastbone.

Then she smiled. That lethal, innocent smile she'd been sporting ever since he'd met her. So, he went straight for her mouth. Maybe to take her perpetual grin—own it.

She didn't think she was the epitome of the hot nanny? *Shit.* She totally was. But not for the usual reasons.

He'd thought of her—under him, on top, on her stomach with her amazing ass in the air. Wet. Always so wet. In the shower. Against the tiles. He'd cradle her head, his knuckles bruising against the tile as he protected the small of her back with his other hand. Let them grow raw in the steam as he smashed her against the back of the shower.

Any man would. Look at her. Empirically, Adelaide was beautiful.

But her appeal was more. It was like she had some strange grasp of his inner world. Knowing when he was a little off, like last night. His daughter was his one soft spot and she knew it.

It should piss him off. Being unreadable was important in his line of work. But somehow, even after only knowing her for a short while, Adelaide sensed the insecurities he carried inside. Oddly, it brought a strange peace. Maybe because she hadn't exploited his weaknesses once they were found. She'd tried to make him feel better, and it worked.

"Should I stop?" he asked into her mouth. He couldn't seem to break the contact.

"No."

"And the whole nailing the hot nanny thing?"

She curled her fists into his shirt, her nails scratching his shoulder blades. "I'm not hot."

She had no fucking idea. "I'm going to have to prove to you how much you are, aren't I?" Then his mouth couldn't stop tasting her, exploring her. His lips slid over hers like he knew they would: as if designed to fit together.

He was probably being an idiot given his whole stay-away-from-women oath. And a woman who worked for him? Not illegal, not even taboo anymore, but it was the exact opposite of why he was here.

Still, this was one rule he had that didn't stand a chance.

Waking up this morning, his arms full of her? His nose full of her scent? His arm ached from his circulation being impinged. It was a small price to pay. She'd fit so beautifully against his side. And again, right now. A perfect fit, especially her mouth.

Being with her like this, with his hands gliding down her back to cup her ass, felt too good, too right, and almost pre-destined. As if he believed in any of that crap.

But one thing he did know: despite any potential gossip,

despite any unknowns about her past life, the evidence was irrefutable. His life—and Maribelle's—had grown better because she was in it.

She abruptly broke the kiss. "This was the hallway where I ran into you that first time. When—"

"I said you weren't going anywhere. I was wrong."

Addy shouldn't go back to that emotional place again—falling for a man she could never have. But he was kissing her. Deeply. With no signs of stopping.

She should stop this. All the reasons they shouldn't be anything but professional with each other stacked up like Jenga blocks.

Ash Scott was out of her league.

He was going back to New York.

How about he was her boss?

But all those facts? *Ashes, ashes, we all crash down.*

She'd spent too much time with kids. As for this adult time she was having now? Reasons be damned. She was so "in."

Please, let him in, her body screamed. For once, she, her mouth, and the rest of her were on the same page. So he broke her heart a trillion years ago? Yes, she could admit it now. But no one should be punished for their past mistakes, especially teenage ones. She was living proof of that one.

Her hands ran up and down the curve of his spine as he arched over her, pressing her against the door of his bedroom. They'd slowly inched their way down the hall toward it. Yet neither one of them seemed to want to stop to open the door.

One of his hands wrapped around the back of her head as if he didn't want it to bang against the hard surface. His other was at the small of her back. She felt completely held. She was literally in the palm of his hands.

His fingers pressed against the crack of her ass and she moaned into his mouth. Her knees ached to spread open. One leg snaked its way up the side of his thigh to hook around his hip. Her fingers moved up along the back of his neck and threaded into his hair.

At this point, her body had a mind of its own. Her hands, mouth, and legs obeyed one thing: a need that rose up like Mt. Vesuvius.

His hand trailed along the back of her thigh and hitched her knee up higher. It was as if they were talking to each other, a back and forth, even though their tongues and lips were definitely preoccupied.

Then, when his captive cock found the most perfect spot? The wicked man bent his knees and then straightened to give her a little more friction. The little noises in her throat turned into a low rumble. That's when his hips began to rock against her a bit. Swear to God she was going to come on the spot.

A loud throat-clearing rang in the air and made them freeze. Someone was in the hallway with them.

He gently let her leg slip down. When he stepped backward, Miss Stevens came into view.

Fan-fricking-tastic. Adelaide brushed her hair off of her face and straightened her T-shirt, which had ridden up her belly considerably.

Ash smirked at her and then slowly turned around. "Yes, Miss Stevens?"

She stood at the end of the hallway for Lord-knows-how-long. The woman was stealthy—and had the *worst* timing.

"Something you need?" he asked casually.

Miss Stevens pursed her lips. "I got your text about

Maribelle. You have an appointment with Dr. Morgansten at 9:30 this morning."

He'd done that last night? When? Probably when she'd fallen asleep—on the job. That's when it hit her. She'd been caught both sleeping *and* slutting on the job.

She should be sorry about it, shouldn't she?

He patted his pockets as if seeking his watch or phone. "What time is it now?"

"8:00. I'm running into town. Back in a bit." Miss Stevens looked at Addy and arched an eyebrow.

Addy tried to scoot by him. "I better go take a shower."

He grasped her arm. "Addy—"

"We don't want to be late."

He dropped his hold. "Yes, you're right. You'll come with us?"

"Of course." Addy smiled at Miss Stevens as she strode by her. The woman did not hide her admonishment.

This hallway was cursed. It had to be.

22

———

Ash studied the back of the children's Tylenol bottle. Now, he and Adelaide were attempting to put Maribelle back to bed. Dr. Morgansten said Maribelle's illness was nothing to worry about, but he was taking no chances.

"But I don't want to take a nap," she whined.

Adelaide pulled the covers up over Maribelle and her doll. "It's not a nap. It's dreamtime. Want me to do the magic thing?"

Maribelle nodded.

Adelaide ran her finger down Maribelle's nose and murmured. Two more strokes and Maribelle's eyes drifted closed. A final nose caress and his little girl was emitting soft snores. Not as loud as an adult man's, but impressive coming from a six-year-old.

"Even her snoring is grown up," Adelaide whispered.

"You read my mind."

"Before you know it, she's going to be dating."

He pulled her away from Maribelle's bed toward the door. "I have at least thirty years before that happens."

She grabbed the baby monitor and waved it at him. "So

we can hear her." The woman really did think of every-thing. "So, thirty years, huh? Please, tell me you're not going to be one of *those* fathers." Her signature smile beamed at him.

He closed the door gently behind them. "I already am." He turned to face her. They needed to talk. "Listen, about…" What could he say? Sorry for ravaging you in the hallway? He wasn't sorry. He didn't know where to go with what they'd started, either.

The last year had been hell, working with people who whispered about you in hallways, seeing headlines on news-stands that mentioned your name, spending time with a six-year-old, always wondering what to say or do. It'd been lonely. Only now he wasn't in it alone anymore, at least, not since Adelaide had semi-moved in.

"So," he tried again, still unsure what to say.

She moved closer to him, sent her hand up to his collar, and straightened it. The simple tug of the fabric around his neck got him hard. "Yes, Mr. Scott?"

She was teasing him.

"Let's start over."

"As in…" Her lashes lifted. Warmth filled her eyes that both made him harder and want to slow down at the same time.

God, he wanted to definitely start over from where they'd left things off outside Maribelle's room, but they had much to discuss first. "After we talk."

He cleared his throat and tilted his hips a bit as if that might make more room in his pants.

He inclined his head. "In my room." The hallway wasn't the place to have the talk they desperately needed to have. That particular part of his house had seen enough action.

He should probably take her to his office and make this conversation professional, but the space was cold, imper sonal. Plus, it was too far away from Maribelle despite the baby monitor Adelaide held.

Once inside his room, he took the plastic monitor from her placed it on the bureau.

He should have settled them in the two wingback chairs by the large bay window that overlooked the back garden. It'd have been safer, sitting across from her than standing so close like they were now at the foot of the bed. But he couldn't seem to make himself lead them over there. His feet remained glued to the floor. Perhaps it was because her hand found its way to his pec.

Warmth seeped through his shirt, and he placed his hand over hers and held it there. Who was he to fight her need to touch him? He couldn't seem to stop himself either.

He ran his hand down her hair, soft and cool like satin. "These last few weeks you've caught me off-guard, Adelaide Bloom. Not many people can do that to me."

"You've done the same."

"But I'm not going to take advantage of you."

She pulled her hand free. "I know." A rare vulnerability flashed across her eyes. "I won't take advantage of you, either." He must have looked puzzled because she explained. "The supermodels? All the women wanting in on your… treasure box."

"Never occurred to me." Not with her, it didn't. One thing he'd learned to do early was judge character. She was too honest, too transparent to be a gold digger. "Rather, I…"

"Having buyer's remorse? I mean, for the earlier kissing?"

"Technically, I haven't bought anything. But no. Quite the opposite."

Her gaze snapped to his. "Oh?"

He nodded. It was true. He'd kiss her again if given the chance. "Not sorry for it. Again."

She ran her finger over the carving in the tall bedpost.

"Well, when you put it that way. I mean, you did miss out a long time ago. But I suppose we could again. I mean, to help you save face for—"

He yanked her close and kissed her. Screw the formality. They could dance around each other for another hour. Truth was his mouth wanted to do more than kiss this woman. He rarely met anyone so guileless. It was damned attractive.

She was a little breathless when he released her a minute later. Just the way he wanted her. "I'm going to have to do that often so I can get a word in edgewise, aren't I?"

She nodded. "Mm-hmm."

"But we need to keep things quiet. Until we…"

"Until I get sick of you?"

He puffed out a laugh "Yeah, until then."

"I can be quiet. Unless…" She played with his collar again. "…you give me a reason to be loud. Want to test it?" she asked quickly, her lips curving upward.

He'd been right about one thing regarding Adelaide: she used that smile—and she used it well. Did he mind? He should, except she wasn't trying to manipulate him.

As for testing how loud she could be? Given how much she could talk, probably pretty damned loud. Thank God old houses had thick walls because nothing interested him more than seeing what decibel level he could raise in this woman.

His hand cupped her cheek and brought her gaze fully to his. "Are you sure?"

"Sure?" She stepped backward and ripped her T-shirt over her head. "I'm not wasting an opportunity to prove to your seventeen-year old self you lost out."

"Well, when you put it that way…" He tugged her closer again so her breasts smashed against his shirt. Her breath warmed his face.

Her fingers fumbled on his shirt buttons. With every button released, any objections he might have had for being with her melted away like snow on a July day. What else was there to say? She was developing some strange hold on his heart, certainly on his libido.

He helped her with the final buttons and ripped his shirt off, probably ruining the cuffs.

But when she tried to pull down her shorts, he stopped her. "We're going to go slow."

Her eyes widened. "You can go fast. I like it."

"No." He pressed her against the solid bedpost, thankful the former occupants enjoyed a sturdy bed. They were going to test the limits of it. "Hold on to the post behind you." She enjoyed taking people off-guard, which put her in charge. Now it was his turn.

He would unwrap her gradually. Reveal her skin inch by inch. Tune into her breathing, watch her pretty lips part as he took control of the situation.

She grasped the wood behind her waist which jutted out her breasts, exactly where he wanted to start.

His hands found her waist as he ravaged her mouth. Once she panted hard into his mouth, he let his hands roam. His fingers trailed up her sides to her bra. He yanked the cups down until her breasts hung heavy over the wire.

"Stay there," he growled. Then he feasted on her. Starting with one nipple, then moving to the next until they stood erect, red as cherries.

"Ash," she whispered.

He got on his knees and moved between her legs. His hands wrapped around her thighs and he pulled, forcing her to widen her legs even more. Then he held her there while he inhaled her scent and tongued her through her shorts until her legs were quivering under her hands.

Her breaths were now audible—raspy little moans that told him everything he needed to know. This woman was going to be loud, alright. Very loud.

He shot to standing, catching her as her knees buckled a little from him no longer holding her upright. He twisted her and bent her over the bed, presenting her perfect behind. Jesus, he might not have been his asshole seventeen-year-old self anymore, but his cock certainly hadn't gotten the memo to grow up. It fought its restriction like a raging beast wanting out, wanting inside her.

Again, why fight it? And by the way her hands clawed at the comforter, her ass pushing back toward him? She wanted him as much as he wanted her.

And God, he more than wanted this woman. He craved her.

He leisurely slipped her shorts and panties down her legs, drinking in the place he was going to spend quite a while on.

Her breath quickened. "Ash, please. Faster."

Fat chance. "Climb up the bed. Get on all fours." They had at least an hour, and he was going to use all sixty minutes of it on her, gorge himself on her.

Ash's tongue should have been patented. He worked her from behind, which was filthy, dirty fabulousness that completely removed any inhibition she might have had about being as naked as a sphynx cat. He'd unhooked her bra and let it fall to her wrists as she stayed on all fours. She was so preoccupied, writhing and keening from his mouth machinations, she'd left it there.

She came *hard.* He didn't stop until she was completely wrung out, now having fallen to her forearms. She only emerged from her coma-gasm when the zip of a zipper being lowered sounded.

She looked over her shoulder because no way was she going to miss out on the sight of him, but she barely got a glimpse before his hands wrapped around himself, pulling on a condom.

He grabbed her hips. "Now ready to go fast?"

She nodded vigorously. He had her flipped over onto her back in seconds. He lifted one of her feet, brought it up to his mouth. He kissed the inside of her arch, then ran his tongue up the inside of her insole.

She was going to levitate to the ceiling. The man was inventing erogenous zones on her.

But then he brought her leg down to his hip, moved forward, and pushed into her so damned slowly her hands grabbed his hips in a vain attempt to pull him inside. There was one zone that needed his full attention.

He tsked. "Trust me."

She did. He wasn't seventeen anymore—not by a long shot. She wasn't that little girl anymore, either. Every cell in their bodies had changed by the time they'd reunited. They were wholly different people. And she was so into this new man, too, especially when he began to thrust inside her, covering her mouth with his lips and holding her hands down by her side.

Her second orgasm did put her on the ceiling. It had to have. But all she remembered was crying out into his mouth.

He wasn't done with her, though. He grasped behind her knees, brought her legs up, and pitched inside her even deeper. The man had some stamina. It was quite a few more minutes before he grunted out his own release and fell on top of her.

He breathed hard into her neck, and a laugh rose up in her throat.

His head lifted. "Something funny?"

"I'm covered in Ash. Both figuratively and literally."

He dropped back down so his face nestled in her neck,

and she wrapped her arms around him. "But not getting dirty," she whispered.

His chest shook as they laughed together. "I'd say you were very, very dirty, Miss Bloom."

"You might have to put me in the shower."

"With pleasure." He eased up. His blue eyes bored down on her. He hesitated, his gaze running over her face and down her neck to her bare breasts. Then, his mouth crashed back down to hers.

They never made it to the shower. Instead, he kissed her for long minutes, slowly and deliberately, until her lips were bruised and the skin around her mouth was abraded from his rough beard.

Yes, this Ash was most definitely not a kid anymore. Everything about him spoke of experience.

When he released her, he still stared at her.

"What?" she asked.

He slowly shook his head. "Nothing. Just admiring."

Finally, he eased himself off, rid himself of the condom—such a mood killer. But then he was back and spooned her from behind where they lay like that, skin cooling, sweat drying, like a couple in a movie scene, on top of his bedcovers.

The old tick-tick-tick of the clock in the hallway joined his heavy breathing. He'd fallen asleep. She didn't mind. It gave her time to think, or rather, relish that she lay in Ash's bed with his arms around her, ruining the duvet cover with all the sexy aftermath.

His last words drifted back to her. *Admiring.* Isn't that what she'd said to him all those years ago?

She played with the hair on his forearm. "Thank you," she whispered.

He shifted, sniffed a little. "For?"

Oh, he was awake. "For not kissing me back then." Her lungs expanded with a big breath.

"I mean, if you had and then gone back to school…" Now that she thought about it, maybe he'd done her a favor. She might have pined for him versus just lusted. That would have been infinitely worse. "Anyway, thanks for waiting."

He chuckled. "Except now that I know you're a stellar kisser, I'm not sure waiting was a wise move."

Such flattery. "I guess that means you can admit you were wrong about me back then."

His low chuckle rumbled through her back. "I was. More than. I actually missed out on something great."

She was woman enough to admit how his words landed. Her ego puffed up like a blowfish—one she wasn't about to deflate. One should never punch a gift horse—or gift fish—in the mouth.

23

————

Ash cracked open his eyes and nearly cried out. Maribelle stared at him, a pink elephant in her arms. She held it up. "Prickly Puss wants pancakes. And then she wants to know if we can build the castle now. She's been waiting *forever*." She dramatically dropped it from view and sighed.

He rolled to his back and his arm pressed against warm flesh. Adelaide.

Oh, shit. They'd fallen asleep. What time was it?

He sat up, the sheet falling across his bare chest. He managed to capture it before it bared any more of Adelaide's skin.

She kicked at the sheets making his efforts moot. Thank Christ, she had on one of his T-shirts. He didn't recall her pulling it on.

She sat up and rubbed her eyes. "Well, I guess you're feeling better, Queen Maribelle."

"My top is itchy. Can I take it off now?"

"Sure thing."

His little girl ran out of the room back to hers. He took

the moment to glance over at Adelaide, who gave him a wide smile. "Told ya' they bounce back fast."

He lowered his voice. "Time to get dressed and out before..." his eyes darted to the doorway Maribelle had disappeared through.

Oooooh, right, she mouthed. She eased herself out of the other side of the bed, taking the sheet with her.

He swung his legs to the floor and maneuvered around an abandoned Prickly Puss, yanked on a pair of sweats and his T-shirt laying across a chair, and picked up the stuffed animal. He turned and Adelaide was gone. Ash grabbed his watch and glanced at it. They'd only been asleep for forty minutes.

He strode down the hall to deposit the stuffed elephant to Maribelle, got her in a "less-itchy" top, and as soon as they stepped out, Adelaide came out of the guest room she'd been sleeping in—or had been—clad in jeans and another T-shirt, pulling her hair up into a messy bun.

Maribelle ran over to her. "Addy, Addy, make your magic pancakes."

Oh, Jesus. Was everything magic around this woman? An inner grin formed inside him. She was a bit magic, he supposed. She'd certainly cast a spell on him.

She placed her hand on Maribelle's forehead as if checking for a fever. "Sounds like a great lunch to me. Fever's all gone, and we need to replenish."

Maribelle took her hand. "I'm glad you slept over again."

He'd never once had a woman around since he and Maribelle had been living together. Maybe he should address it. "Maribelle, about—"

"The pancakes." Addy widened her eyes at him. "I'm thinking banana nut over blueberry. You?"

Maribelle jumped up and down. "With chocolate chips!"

"Maybe," he said, more than a little relieved Maribelle

seemed more interested in sugar than his and Adelaide's "sleepover." Having to address it wasn't going to be his favorite topic.

Yet as they took the stairs down, all he could think about what how one addressed the bird and the bees with kids.

A memory thunked from the sky and made his jaw ache a little. His father had given him "the talk" decades ago. Right before Ash had left for boarding school. It was wrapped up in other tenets like Ash would be expected to "man up" at school. There also was "no tears for the weak" and other platitudes shared.

He was how old? Eight? Of course, there were tears. Even from his mother. He sucked in a long breath. He'd forgotten that—how his mother hadn't wanted him to go and his father couldn't get him out the door fast enough.

Adelaide patted his arm as she snuck by him in the kitchen door. "I think we should add sausages, too. You're going to need your strength to build that tree castle today."

He cocked an eyebrow. "Is that what I'm doing?" Maribelle beamed up at him, her eyes full of hope. He lifted her up into his arms. "Yeah, guess I am."

She wrapped hers around his neck and squeezed him. Maybe he'd build her a two-story with an actual turret.

Adelaide straightened Maribelle's top. "Ash Scott, I knew you had a knight in you."

This woman knew how to play to his ego alright.

"Like the Princess movie castle, Daddy."

Ash sat at the old farmhouse table with Maribelle, sketching on a napkin.

Addy pointed at the junk drawer she'd found some time

ago looking for a tea strainer. "I think there's paper in that drawer."

He waved his pen in the air. "The greatest ideas are always on napkins. Southwest Airlines, *Toy Story*…"

She pointed her spatula at him. "I'm surprised you've ever seen *Toy Story*."

He chuffed. "Not *Hamlet*, but it had its moments." His phone buzzed on the table. He glanced at it and tapped on it then set it back down. She didn't get a clear line of sight to the screen, but she'd suspiciously noted the name started with S. Maybe Stevens?

"Hey, where's Miss Stevens? Maybe she wants some."

"Told her to take the weekend off. Let's see if she manages it."

She dropped a dollop of batter in the oil and it sizzled. Perfect. "Why wouldn't she? Does she work weekends a lot?"

"In our line of business, any day is a workday."

"Yeah, mine, too." His brow crinkled as if concerned, which was rich given the man was a workaholic himself. "Kids need care all the time. As a relief nanny, I often worked weekends and nights."

She dropped another spoonful of batter onto the oil to a delightful sizzle. His phone buzzed again. Behind her, she heard the scrape of it being lifted and then placed back down on the table. It made her insides a little giddy that he was ignoring calls while being with her and Maribelle.

She flipped the first pancake. "So, about the first day of school in a few days…"

The scrape of a chair sounded. Ash joined her by the stove.

"I'm thinking the yellow ribbon." He sipped his coffee and winked at her over the coffee cup. "But why don't we let Maribelle decide?"

Her eyebrows shot up. "Seriously?"

"I'll decide that morning, Daddy," Maribelle said.

"How about the night before?" Addy scooped out three of the pancakes with the flipper and put them on the warm plate by the stove. It was already stacked with a dozen pancakes.

"But I won't know what mood I'm in until I wake up."

"She really is six going on forty-five, you know?" she whispered to the girl's father.

"Don't remind me." He took the plate and put it on the table.

Addy moved to join them. This time when his phone ran, she clearly saw who was calling. "Albrecchio" displayed across the screen.

Ash noticed she noticed. "She's been calling for some reason."

"Probably wants to check in on our latest *Moorsvillian.*"

He snorted out a laugh. "I'm sure she would like to. Check me out."

"She wanted to be an actress once. Maybe she wants your contacts." She moved to the refrigerator. Pancakes demanded ice-cold milk to accompany them.

"Is that right?" He opened a cabinet and took out plates. "She didn't mention that."

"Yeah. She went to L.A. Or so I heard. Lasted a year. Got tired of waitressing, I guess. So, she came back." Addy lowered her voice as if they'd have a chance Maribelle might not hear. "She was the most beautiful girl in town for years She thought it'd be enough in L.A."

"I've heard that story before." He leaned a hip against the counter. "But with you in town, I'm not sure how anyone could claim the top beauty spot."

Now it was her turn to snort. "You just want access to my pancakes." She pointed down at the batter. She could make a dozen more if needed.

"Oh, I want access alright."

His gaze caught hers. He ensnared women with those eyes. He certainly always had done that to her. And now? Totally caught. However, this time, no matter what he did, she knew she could survive it. She was nothing if not resilient.

"I do feel bad for Sally sometimes." Addy did—some days. Insecurity had to be at the root of her haughtiness. "It's hard to lose your dreams." Still, she wouldn't grow hard like Sally did when things didn't work out.

"It is." Ash leaned against the counter, staring at Maribelle. Was he having yet another worry moment for his daughter? He didn't need to. He had more of the fatherhood thing down than most of the family's she'd worked with.

"Can we have chocolate chip next?" Maribelle stuffed a too-large piece of pancake in her mouth.

"No," she and Ash said in unison.

"That's a surprise," Ash said. "Agreeing with me on something sweet?"

She eyed him. "It's only because we're out of them."

His phone rang yet another time. This time, he held the off button for a long second until it went dark. "Let's say we go the lumberyard next."

"You're serious."

"Deadly." He raised his voice. "So, Maribelle…" He joined her at the table. "What do you say we start on your tree house? When you're done."

She gasped and dropped her fork with a clatter against the plate. She scooted off her chair. "I'm done. Let's go. And I want a moat."

"I heard moats are out of fashion," Addy said. "How about a garden with all kinds of flowers?"

She cocked her head and thought for a minute. "Like daisies. The yellow kinds with black middles."

"Black-Eyed Susans?"

Ash stilled. His smile dropped.

"Something wrong?" she asked him.

"No." He shook his head. "No, nothing." He intertwined his hand with hers. "Want to build a tree house with me?"

"Castle. And yes, I'd love to build it with you."

She could do this—help him and Maribelle grow closer. It felt good to be part of his family. She sucked in a long breath and told herself to chill. She was getting ahead of herself. They'd had one night together.

But then Ash lifted her hand and kissed her knuckles—in front of Maribelle.

Addy thought for sure Ash would hire an architect for Maribelle's tree castle. At least a builder or team of work-men. Turned out the man not only knew his way around a lumberyard but he had some building skills. Right there, in the middle of the lumber section of Build Center, he sketched out the rough plan of what he wanted. Two men with arms crossed nodded their heads in agreement.

She wanted to have a moment to think about last night, about how she'd gone so quickly from wondering if he liked her at all to basically calling out his name while yanking on his hair. But every time she did, the soreness between her legs ached—as in "not-sore-enough-wanna-go-again?"

Within an hour, his SUV was filled to the brim with hickory planks sticking out the back along with a miter saw, boxes of nails and a nail gun, angle braces, and other pieces and parts. The rest of the lumber would be delivered later that afternoon, but he had enough to at least get started.

As soon as they got home, she helped him unload all the makings of one tree castle under the old oak tree. Maribelle and Prickly Puss "supervised."

Then, he went straight to work.

Two hours into the project, Addy revised her thoughts on Ash's hottest moments. Watching him with Maribelle was heartwarming. Watching him bent over a saw, cutting wood, while wearing a pair of safety glasses? Total lady boner material.

She helped hold some of the wood pieces so her hands—and imagination—had something to do while Maribelle sat a fair distance away with her dolls on a blanket in "management." Prickly Puss was the lead supervisor and only given the job because Miss Charlotte was "exhausted" from the day.

Delegating suited Maribelle. She was going to lead a company one day, wasn't she?

"Don't you want to take a break?" she asked Ash.

He straightened, then bent backward to stretch out his back. "Maybe for a quick second." They glanced over at Maribelle. She'd fallen asleep on the blanket. "You want to address last night."

Not a question, a statement. "Yes. About that. I don't normally do that kind of thing."

"I know." He swiped the ends of his shirt over his face, gathering sweat. She tried hard not to stare at his abs. And failed, of course. "I don't either."

"So…" She didn't quite know where to go with this conversation. "The thing is, we don't know each other that well. I mean, I usually need to know your mother's maiden name before even considering—"

"Pritchett."

Her lips parted and she cocked her head.

"My mother's maiden name." He grinned at her. "Yours? I mean, fair is fair."

"Bigsley. Don't laugh."

"Wouldn't dream of it. What else do you want to know?"

He was serious. "How do you know how to do this?" Addy waved around the small construction pile strewn about the yard. Building wasn't exactly a skill she'd believe Ash had.

"I did a few summers doing construction. Don't all teenage boys?"

"Not ones named Ash Scott."

"Well, this one did. Hated every second of it. Penance laid down by my father."

She didn't know much about Mr. Scott senior except he always seemed to be working—like his son. "He made you work construction? I always assumed you spent your entire summer playing polo or sailing." A little clichéd of her to think so, but her mind had to fill in the gaps of what she knew.

"In order for me to play on weekends, I had to work for some of his real estate projects during the week. It was the deal. Something about making me into a man."

She swiped hair off her damp forehead. "It worked."

"Glad to hear you think so." He glanced over at Maribelle. "I'd say other things helped in that department."

Oh, melt her clothes right off her body, why didn't he? "So, you and your dad built that first tree house?" She pointed to the pile of old wood he'd excavated from the pitiful structure that had once stood in this tree. It was the first thing he did. He tore down the pieces like a man possessed.

"No, my grandfather built that for my dad."

"Oh." That's right. The Scott mansion had seen five generations of Scotts over the years.

"Though, he didn't spend much time in it."

"Workaholic like you?"

"You could say that. 'Recreation is for the weak,' he'd say." He grinned at her. "I still used to come here. Hide out. Read."

"I'm sorry we couldn't salvage it then." If it was a favorite childhood place, it must have been hard to dismantle it.

"Nah. Good riddance."

"Not sentimental about the past, huh?"

"Not in the slightest."

That was good because Addy couldn't ever seem to get away from hers—not in Moorsville anyway. But where would she go if not here? Even though her and Scarlett's parents passed a few years ago, the old caretaker still worked the family farm in exchange for living there in perpetuity. And Addy could never leave her sister.

"When it's time to let go, it's time to let go."

Her neck prickled oddly at his words. "Some things are worth hanging on to."

He didn't answer, rather picked up two pieces of wood and measured an angle brace against them.

Maybe she'd hit a nerve. It made her sad that he didn't have summers of whacking a polo ball with one of those long mallets to the cheers of fans every day. Or hoisting up sails in his bathing suit and polo shirt while bikini-clad women ooh-ed and ahh-ed over him.

Okay, maybe not have the girls swooning all over him, their legs tan and toned from… whatever rich girls did. But she definitely wished he'd had more fun in his life. Surely, he'd had some given the number of trophies of his that she'd dusted years ago.

"Other than hanging out in your tree house and working construction, and the polo weekends, what else did you do for fun?"

He kept his eye on the angle brace. "Hold this for me while I nail it in place."

She did and startled when the nail gun went off. She glanced at Maribelle, who was now awake and putting together her "puzzle cookies," the broken pieces that Addy told her had to be reassembled before eating. It kept her occupied.

"Well, Scarlett and I used to play in this creek. Catch the minnows and make leaf boats. And horseback riding on the trails."

"Sounds great." He hoisted the wood up so it stood like a triangle in the yard.

She mock-punched him. "You can admit it. It sounds sad to you, doesn't it?"

"No, it sounds…" He looked up at the back of the house, rising so tall it blocked half the sunlight across the backyard. "Free."

He seemed to shake off whatever dark thought crossed his eyes in that moment. She tried to do the same with the pang of sorry that arrowed through her belly.

"Hey, I have an idea. Let's throw a party back here. Unveil the tree castle." She widened her arms to frame the tree trunk. "Show off your mad skills."

He stilled. "Maybe. I'm going to have to head back up to New York soon. I've been away for two weeks, and the natives are growing restless."

"Oh, sure."

"Once Maribelle is in school, I'll be heading up there more and more. Not much time for parties, I'm afraid."

There was a message in his words. She could feel them more than hear them. He was warning her. Last night was fun, but he wasn't about that, was he?

That's when it hit her. He'd moved the conversation away from last night with ease. Man, he was good.

Maribelle appeared. "Are you done with the loud stuff yet?"

He smiled down at her. "No more sawing. Now we hammer."

She brightened. "Can I do it?"

"I'm afraid not, Belle."

"But you can help paint it yellow, right?" Addy asked.

Ash didn't look like he was sold on that idea.

"What? It's not like getting dirty," she teased. So she lied a bit there as paint was nearly impossible to get out of hair, which would inevitably happen.

"We'll see. I distinctly recall paint fumes not being good for children."

Ah, the famous *Genius Child* book. There was a whole section of chemicals to keep away from children. He hadn't raised the book in a while. She'd secretly hoped he'd abandoned its premises altogether. *Ha.*

"But we're outside," she said.

"I'll think about it. Now, we have to get this foundation done. We have a deadline." He stared hard at Addy.

Ah, school. It started on Monday. At least, she hoped that was the only deadline he was thinking about. Her stomach flipped anyway in warning.

25

A long line of SUVs snaked slowly around the avenue leading up to the school.

Ash set his elbow on the door ledge. "Jesus. Please, tell me it's not going to be like this every day."

Addy leaned her head against her headrest. "It's going to be worse. The novelty will have worn off."

"No novelty to begin with."

She swiveled her head to face him. "I can take her if you don't want to."

"No, I can do it."

He sounded so vehement it caught her off-guard.

Addy had to keep reminding herself it had nothing to do with her. He was about to send his little girl to school for the first time. It messed with parents. She'd seen it time and again.

Besides, she was still in his bed every night.

After their non-talk while he built Maribelle's tree house, it simply was never brought up again. They'd tuck Maribelle in at night, and somehow, she ended up naked in his bed. She wasn't sorry one bit. Being with Ash was the best sex of her life. Even if she'd had to do the walk of shame through the hallway the last two mornings to not alert Maribelle where she was every night, being with him was worth it.

Adelaide turned in her seat to look at Maribelle, whose eyes were darting around the scene outside the window. Children of all ages were hopping out of backseats, backpacks jostling on their little bodies as they sauntered up the long sidewalk leading to the school. Two boys, looking about ten years old, greeted each other with big smiles and slaps to their packs.

They'd got a late start since Queen Maribelle couldn't decide which ribbon to wear, the yellow one or the white one with yellow butterflies. She kept wanting to change it. Addy recognized the delaying tactic. Eventually, she was convinced to choose—yellow, of course—when Ash said he would be the one to take her first-grade picture.

She posed like a pro with the little chalkboard Addy had picked up announcing her first day of school. Still, she wasn't looking confident.

Addy sent her hand back to touch Maribelle's leg. "Cloak on?"

She nodded. "I think we should go back and get Miss Charlotte."

"Remember, we said we'd have to leave your animals and dolls at home, right?"

Ash lifted his chin and peered up into his rearview mirror. "They'll be waiting for you when you get home, and you can tell them all the stories about school."

"But Miss Charlotte is miffed she's missing out."

Ash wrinkled his brow and glanced at Addy. "Miffed?"

"They're sponges at this age. She must have heard you use the word."

"I'd use something stronger, but let's not go there." He

finally was able to pull up to the drop-off curb. He cracked open his door, and she did the same.

Maribelle peered around the edge of her car seat out the window. She was nervous, very nervous. It was understandable, but it worried Addy. She'd been through this a thousand times, so why was her stomach jumping around like it was practicing grand jetés?

They both opened the car doors to the back seat at the same time. Maribelle looked back and forth like she didn't know which exit to take.

Addy smiled and gently closed her door to walk to Ash's side. This was his first day, too. He'd likely have Addy drop her off every day from now on anyway.

He had a bit of trouble getting Maribelle out of her car seat, which was strange. Hadn't he done this before? Soon Maribelle wouldn't need to be in one at all, though, which made Addy's heart squeeze a little.

She shook it off. It was her job to help them move through various stages of Maribelle growing up, to be strong.

Adelaide and Ash each took one of Maribelle's hands to walk her up the sidewalk.

A group of women was standing around the entrance, chatting away. When one of them, a woman with long red hair, stepped to the side, Sally Albrecchio's horse face beamed through the klatch. *Great.*

She wouldn't let the woman spoil Maribelle's first day. Her father was feeling pretty good about his sense of fatherhood now that he'd half-built a tree castle for his daughter. And Addy and Ash were… a thing. A very good thing.

Sally smiled and nodded once her way, then darted through the knot of women like a shark splitting a school of fish. She marched right up to them.

"Why, hello. Happy first day of school." The woman didn't even look down at Maribelle.

"Welcoming the little Moorsvillians to school?" Addy asked cheerily. She was surprised she didn't gag on her own words. But again, good mood intact.

Ash held out his hand to her and Sally's smile dropped. "Ms. Albrechhio. Nice to see you again."

Sally returned the handshake, clearly dismayed by this turn of events. Addy couldn't have been more proud of the man. He didn't lead anyone on. So, she guessed that was good?

A woman in a finely cut red suit waved at them and headed their way. She must have been new to town because Adelaide didn't recognize her at all. What had happened to this place? Gone for one whole summer and the entire population was turning over.

"Hello, Mr. Scott. So good to see you again. And Mrs. Scott?" She held out her hand to Adelaide.

Sally cackled. "Oh, no, Principal Johnson. This is Ash's nanny. Addy."

"I see. You look like a team."

Ashton laughed. A *real* laugh.

"Something funny?" Adelaide asked.

He pursed his lips and gave a tight shake of his head. "As you probably heard, Principal Johnson, it's just Maribelle and I at home so… Miss Bloom was good enough to help us out recently."

Help him out?

"Yes, she's very helpful," Sally muttered. "But Mr. Scott is very hands-on with his daughter. I've seen it. Will *Miss Bloom* also be part of the drop-off and pick-up team? We'd need to sign some paperwork to make sure she's allowed, of course."

Ash nodded. "Of course."

Did they not get Addy was standing right here? "And what are you doing, Sally? Hanging out at school?"

"All the board members come on the first day to greet the

students." She gave Maribelle a forced smile. "Ready for your big day?"

Maribelle bit her bottom lip and grew closer to Addy.

"Maribelle was born ready."

"Oh, yes, you do believe children are born with everything." She waved her hand in the air. "But we at the academy make sure they *have* everything they need for the real world. If it wasn't for my time here, I dare say I'd end up as a waitress. And you," she bent at the waist toward Maribelle, "were made for great things."

She had that right.

Sally straightened and stared straight at Adelaide. "Not everyone is."

Addy's fists curled, and she literally bit down on the tip of her tongue to keep the tirade growing inside her from unleashing. This was Maribelle's day, she reminded herself.

"Finding one's niche is important," Ash agreed. "Let's go, Maribelle. Go find your classroom."

"I want Addy to come." She slipped her little hand into Addy's, which she squeezed in solidarity.

"We find that it's best to only have one parent deliver the child to the classroom," Ms. Johnson said.

"Oh, no problem then." Sally practically clapped her hands in glee. "Ash is the only parent here."

Way to overstep your boundaries there. Addy crouched down to Maribelle. "You got this, Queen Maribelle."

Her little forehead crinkled and she bit her lip. Addy straightened the shoulders on her top. "Right?" she asked, hoping Maribelle would remember her magic invisible cloak if needed.

Maribelle took in a long breath and nodded once.

Addy straightened and came face to face with Ash's hand dangling his car keys as if he were handing them over to a valet. "Mind moving my car for me? We'll be out in a second."

What the…? Then Sally began to walk with them. She tried to grasp Maribelle's hand, who jerked it away to place both in her father's.

Good girl. Keep those instincts. As for her own? They clearly weren't firing on any cylinders. She was the nanny. He was the parent. And he didn't want anyone to know about them any differently.

Half of her argued it was appropriate. He'd promised her nothing. And his daughter shouldn't be caught in between them.

The other half of her? It screamed like a petulant child wanting attention. She hated being the lover he was keeping secret.

Ash didn't return from delivering Maribelle to class for thirty minutes. She'd gone through everything in her purse just to have something to do. She almost dialed Scarlett twenty times but stopped because she didn't want to get caught in mid-rant if he came back suddenly. Now, she chewed her fingernail and waited.

She sucked at waiting.

Finally, he emerged from the front entrance. Sally clung to his arm, the parasite. He was laughing down at her. Even from where Addy sat, she could make out the fire in his blue eyes. Eerily familiar fire. He'd looked at her that way.

She sat up straighter in the passenger seat. She hadn't moved the car—hadn't needed to given they were one of the last few cars to drop off a child.

Ash ran a hand through his gorgeous dark hair, and Sally bit her lip. Addy wasn't a jealous person—usually. What were they talking about?

He finally glanced her way and lifted his chin. Oh, look. An acknowledgement of her existence. How positively sweet and kind of him, the fool.

He held out his hand in a handshake for Sally and they

parted. She almost moved to get the hand sanitizer out of her purse for him but resisted the urge.

He climbed into the front seat. "Didn't need to move her?" He sounded downright cheery.

Maribelle rose in her mind immediately. "No. How was she? Did she cry? Did it take long for her to get settled?"

He looked aghast. "No. She ran to the first group of girls she saw."

"Oh, thank God." She threw her head against the headrest. "It's important to make friends right away. She looked good, didn't she? The yellow ribbon?"

"Uh-huh." Ash stared over the schoolyard to where Sally stood. He seemed lost in thought.

"So." Addy reached for her seatbelt. "Sally…"

Ash didn't answer.

"She ask you out again?"

"No." He still hadn't looked at her. He started up his car and got his seatbelt on.

Addy reached for hers. She tried to get the metal piece to fit into the buckle but it wouldn't go in for some reason. "But did she say anything—"

"It's nothing, Adelaide."

Oh, stern voice.

Addy continued to try to click her seatbelt secure but now it stuck three inches too short. She let it go and yanked it back down. "Nothing, huh?" She tried to sound light but it came out in a frustrated growl. Metal clanked against metal. Stupid seatbelt. It still wouldn't go in. She finally let it slide back from where it came.

Ash glanced over at her. "What's wrong with you?"

She twisted in her seat. "What's really going on?"

"Nothing." He waved his hand. "I won't let Sally get any wrong ideas."

"So, you *did* say something to her."

He dipped his head a little to see a traffic light. "No."

"You can't stop gossip, you know. And the best way to end gossip? Tell the truth."

He sat back and rested his wrist casually on the steering wheel. "You mean about us. Do you want that?"

"No. I mean, it's no one's business, but…"

"But what?"

"I don't know." She really didn't. For such a simple scenario, things got complicated fast.

It was the stress of Maribelle's first day, she told herself. That's what had her so tense. The problem was, why wasn't Ash? Unless he was once again stuffing everything down. Or he had gotten reassurance from Sally. That last possibility? Irritated her to no end.

They drove back to his house in silence.

As soon as they stepped into the entranceway of his house, he turned to her. "I have to get some work done…"

"Oh, sure. I'll go straighten up Maribelle's room." It'd been sadly neglected, too. Maribelle was a bit of a slob.

"Why don't you take the day off?"

A tiny electric shock ran up her legs. "Oh, no, I—"

"You've been working hard."

"Working," she measured. "Yes. Okay. Well, should I be back to help you pick her up?"

He winked at her, an impersonal "gotcha" kind of move. "No, I can do that."

The earlier electric shock? It travelled straight to her heart which now punched at her ribcage like it wanted out. He then gave her a view of his wide back.

She tapped on the door jamb of his office, searching for words. Questions mounted on her tongue.

He turned his attention to his desk. Lifted a file folder. He didn't seem to notice at all when she turned to leave.

She could get a clue. Maribelle officially was in school. He had been ignoring his office. But he'd denied their bond…

Bond. Listen to yourself, girl.

Instead of turning right to go upstairs, she turned left and immediately out the front door. A day off sounded good because something most definitely went down a few minutes ago, and it wasn't good.

She'd been a fool about Ash Scott again, hadn't she?

26

———

Scarlett forked the apple pie straight out of the tin. Peppermint Sweet was quiet, thank goodness.

Between chews, she'd listened to Adelaide tell her every detail of the last forty-eight hours. She'd left out the sexy parts. Or, as Scarlett said, "left out the good bits, which is so unfair."

No, what was unfair was Ash running hot and cold on her.

Scarlett slipped the fork between her lips. "It's because he likes you. Like *really* likes you. That's why he's acting weird. He doesn't know what to do with it."

"But I thought we were heading somewhere."

Scarlett dipped her chin and peered at Addy from hooded eyes as if to say, *'You total moron. We're talking Ash Scott.'* "You mean fall completely in love with you like you are with him?"

Scarlett always did get right to the point. "Yes." Why deny it?

In the last few weeks, her heart had burst out of its usual, logical place, mowed down every red flag in its wake, and barreled straight into the proverbial sunset with dreams of soul mate love. She didn't know exactly when or how her heart escaped her chest, but now it lay in a field of hearts and cupids waiting for Ash to fall down with her. Like the *Twilight* movie where the vampire and innocent stared at each other in a field of purple flowers.

She was screwed. *Dammit.* She was smarter than this.

The pie pan scraped across the glass countertop as Scarlett pushed it away. "Has it ever occurred to you he's fighting his feelings for you?"

Her neck nearly snapped as her chin jutted backward. "And why would he do that?"

"Because you're nothing like he expected." She raised her palm up. "High five. Adelaide Bloom does it again."

Addy gave her a half-hearted slap back. "I don't know what you're talking about."

Scarlett pointed her fork at her. "You were more than he could have possibly dreamed of."

Addy chortled. "Yeah, right. I basically broke all of his rules…"

"All?" Scarlett raised one eyebrow.

"Okay, not all but many. I hit the man with water balloons. Maribelle may never put another dress on—"

"That's awesome. Patriarchy holdover."

"I practically forced him into building a tree castle. And then there was the dry humping in the hallway where we got caught by Miss Stevens. Then, later—"

"Now we're getting somewhere with this conversation. Before you spill the very fine details you owe your sister, are we talking about *the* famous hallway?"

"The very one."

"Huh. That's smart. Screw the bad ju-ju right out of that place." She sent her gaze to the ceiling in thought.

Whoever finally landed Scarlett was going to have one

fun life ride. Too bad Ash didn't seem to want to stay on Addy's fun ride.

She huffed and put her chin in her hands. "I need to figure out what to do next. Take charge of the situation."

"Revisit the hallway."

"What?"

"I have a sense about these things. You do, too. It's a Bloom trait. Go back there and ask the hallway."

Addy chuckled. "Ask the hallway?"

"Look, it's the place of every big happening in your life."

"Well, not every happening."

Scarlett gave her the side-eye again but then straightened. "Isn't Mrs. Scott's portrait in that corridor?"

Addy's mind searched for the visual. She thought she knew every inch of the place but, like most homes, one stops seeing things after a while. Mrs. Scott's kind, small smile formed in her mind. She wore a blue dress in that picture. It was in a gold oval frame hung over a console table with a small lamp.

She snapped her fingers. "You're right."

Scarlett grasped Addy's shoulder. "So, go ask her what your next move should be. Like a self-therapy exercise."

"Something tells me she's got fewer words for me than Ash does right now."

"Then you're going to have to take my words to heart. He doesn't know what to make of his good fortune. Betcha he doesn't trust it. Give the man time. Now… chocolate crème next? It'll go well with all the humping details you're about to give me."

According to Scarlett, today was "pie-tasting" day where she had to try all the flavors Peppermint Sweet had on hand that day. "No thanks, and you'll have to live without any more details. Listen, I'm going to go back."

"There's my girl. Let me know what Mrs. Scott says," she whispered dramatically.

She hugged her sister. She was crazy, but Addy loved her. And no one loved Addy as much as Scarlett. As for Ash? Did the man even know how to love, now that she thought about it? He'd never been married. Had been with a woman every night of his life if the tabloids had any truth to them at all. Maybe Scarlett was right. He didn't know what to do with her—or his interest in her.

She left Peppermint Sweet and drove straight back to the Scott Mansion. Ash wasn't in his office. She wasn't ready to see him anyway.

Her legs got her up the stairs, and somehow, she found herself exactly where Scarlett had directed her to go.

She paused in front of Mrs. Scott's portrait. It was smaller than she recalled, classier. Swipes of oil paint created a light halo around her head. Her perfectly coiffed blond hair curled around her face. The painter did a good job, catching her sly smile which always made you wonder what she was thinking. Kind of like Ash.

"Well, here I am. Ready to talk to a portrait." She twisted her fingers together. "So, Mrs. Scott. First, I never thanked you for helping me back then. Or maybe I did. I can't remember. Anyway, thanks for being so nice to me. And for helping me get over Bryson."

That was something she hadn't told Ash, how his mother was pivotal to standing up for herself when most of the town chose his side of things when his cheating was brought to light.

"I could use your help. It's your son, Ash." Addy sent her gaze down at the carpeting. She felt like an idiot. She hadn't been this off-balance since… Bryson.

After a few deep breaths, she set her sights back on the painting. "First, thanks for having him. He's… great. A little acerbic at times." That was a word Ash would use. Man, he was rubbing off on her. "But he has a kind heart."

She raised a hand. "And you'd have loved Maribelle. In fact," she lowered her voice and leaned closer, "I think maybe she's channeling you."

Mr. Scott may have made all the money in the family. But Mrs. Scott? That woman ran things, as in every last activity and detail inside this house was chosen by her. No one complained. No one questioned her. Kind of like Maribelle.

"She's so lovely." Gah, her voice cracked, a weird emotion creeping up on her. She cleared her throat. "A queen. And I love her." Oh, man, she was going to cry. In front of a painting, of all things.

She shook her hair out of her face, "I'm here to ask you something. Should I stay or should I go? Am I being a fool about Ash? Or taking a good chance? Does he really, really like me? Or just want my rocking body?" She threw in a little sarcasm at the end.

Naturally, no answer.

"Maybe if I was more stately, like you… Not that it would ever work. Or maybe if I was more like a supermodel… That wouldn't work, either." She snorted and her shoulders dropped. "I mean, can you imagine me trying to put on false eyelashes?"

"No, I can't."

She almost jumped out of her skin. She twisted and bumped against the console table. The lamp tipped and she had to throw out her arms to catch it.

Ash quickly moved closer to her. "They look like insects crawling on a woman's face. Not a fan of them." He glanced up at the painting of his mother and pointed at it. "What are you doing?"

"I was just saying hi to your mom." Oh yeah, that sounded sooo good.

He chuckled a little. "Oh? How is she?"

"Fine. Fine." Okay, now she was channeling Ash. "What are *you* doing?" He wore shorts and a T-shirt with a big sweat stain down the middle of his chest.

"Missed my morning run thanks to a certain brunette in my bed."

She flushed even though who would blame her for her actions that morning? When one wakes up against a chest like his, well, it kind of demands she climb up on top of it to do… things.

He stared down at her. "I thought you were going to take the day off."

"Is that what you were hoping I'd do? Leave?"

"Thought you'd appreciate it. Having a little bit of time to yourself."

Oh, when he put it that way. "Is that what you need?" She hated how desperate she sounded. This was not her at all.

He cocked his head and an understanding filled his eyes. "Anything you want to ask me?"

"Oh no. Nothing at all." Now she sounded like Minnie Mouse. Why was this so hard?

"You know, for someone who uses a lot of words, you seem to be a little short of them now." He took her hand. "I think I know what's going on here. You want to ask me about us, don't you?"

He probably recognized it. How many women had he had to field questions from? A thousand?

She rolled her lips between her teeth and nodded.

He reached over and ran his thumb across her lips, releasing them. "This is what I can tell you. I don't know. My life is complicated. But I care about you. I want you here. With me. Can that be enough for now?"

"Yes." It was. He was being honest with her. And she'd rushed to some conclusions, which wasn't fair.

"Now, I do have to get back to work. But first, a shower."

"Oh, okay." She stepped back to let him pass.

He didn't move. Rather, he held out his hand in invitation. "Care to join me?"

His blue eyes sparkled, and for once, they weren't pools of ice or fire. They'd softened as if uncertain, which nearly undid her altogether. He was hoping she'd take his hand, wasn't he?

She took his fingers, but then he yanked her closer and tossed her over her shoulder. She squealed. He slapped her ass, and a stuttered chortle erupted from her throat. "Hey, caveman…"

"We have the house to ourselves. Time to see how loud you can be."

He had no idea what he was in for.

Her view of the room bounced as he carried her to the bathroom. Okay, distraction sex was about to ensue. She supposed it was better than stewing about all the *what ifs*.

He set her down, and she spit hair out of her face. He reached over to turn on the shower water, grinning from ear to ear.

As he moved, his pec muscles punched through the fabric of his T-shirt. Like seriously fighting the restriction. As soon as he straightened, she wasted no time yanking it up. Who was she to let a fight between manly muscle and fabric continue?

"Off with you," she whispered. This was most definitely better than worrying about their future.

He chuckled and yanked it over his head. He drew down his shorts, and holy mother, the man was happy to see her.

His gaze drifted down to her legs, up her torso, and back to her face. "Do you want to remove your jeans or shall I?"

Oh, she'd kind of frozen—like a possum staring down a

wolf. He had a wild, feral look in his eyes. *Yay.* Bring on the feral wolf.

She had her jeans unbuttoned, unzipped, and down her legs in a nanosecond. "I guess I don't have the patience you do." She furiously kicked them off and stood there in her bra and panties, waiting for his wolfish side to pounce. "Okay, ready."

He chuckled. "Once more, I appreciate your enthusiasm."

His fingertip traced along her shoulder to her bra strap and brought it down to her elbow. He did the same with the other. It was maddeningly slow but sent shivers dancing across her skin.

After that? Let's say she didn't recall how she got her bra and panties off—or exactly how they got into the shower. Or how he got a condom on himself. Or how the heck it stayed on in the shower. Or…

His mouth latched onto hers and pushed her deeper into the warm spray that fell over them. Cold tile hit her back, but her front was as hot as pavement under a summer sky. His hands wrapped around her thighs, inched around, and then yanked one up so she could wrap it around his waist.

He entered her—slowly. So fucking slowly she was going to lose her mind.

Then, she kind of did—and she let it out. She bit into his shoulder and he grunted. But his hips finally moved, and her voice bounced off the tile. For once, he didn't seem to mind that she was loud.

27

———

Addy woke with a start when she heard a loud bang downstairs. She'd fallen asleep on his bed.

Ash was right about one thing. She hadn't had much time off. Now, with a few hours to herself, not to mention some of the best shower sex she'd ever had, fatigue took her over.

The last thing she remembered was watching him pull clothes over his finely chiseled body. The one that made her come twice in the shower. She could go again in a nanosecond if—she sat up—he was here.

And there she went again—total lust monkey. It was because the sheet clinging to her nude body smelled like him.

Where was he?

A quick glance at the clock revealed they had some time before Maribelle needed to be picked up. She still couldn't believe they'd kept her for a whole day on her first day. The Moorsville Girls Academy wasn't kidding about "preparing them for the real world." The little girl would need a nap after today, too.

Addy reached down and grabbed one of Ash's abandoned T-shirts. The man needed a maid to follow him around given the trail of stuff he left behind him. Ash was a bit of a slob now that she took in some of the details of the room.

He didn't make his bed. A pillow lay on the floor next to the bed. A bottle of water with the cap off stood on the nightstand. A pair of trousers that was tossed over the back of a wingback chair.

Ash also was kinder than she expected. He also wasn't afraid to talk to her once she let her own guard down.

She twisted her hair up with a hair tie and headed downstairs. Halfway down the stairs, she stopped short.

He stood in the open doorway, staring at something in his hand. He glanced up at her and lifted the bottles in his hand. "Someone left these on the front stoop for you."

She drew closer and read one of the notes attached by a piece of raffia string as if it were from a fancy spa. "It's to me."

Remember where you came from. ~S.

Then she saw the contents. *Oh, shit. Oh, shit. Oh, shit.*

"Who would send you jalapeno juice?" Ash asked.

Damn Sally. For someone in her late thirties, she was so immature. Then again, Addy hadn't been the bastion of maturity all the time. *Gah, please, don't ask me about what you found, Ash.*

He peered outside. "I don't see anyone."

"Maybe just a prankster." She yanked the two bottles from his grasp. 'I'll pop these to the kitchen." And down the drain.

His brow wrinkled. He was worried. "Still… strange."

"People around here have a strange sense of humor."

Stevens peeked her head out of his office. "Mr. Scott." Her gaze ran over Addy, who stood there in a long T-shirt and no pants, but then back up to Ash. "It's New York again."

"Thought she was off today?" she whispered to Ash.

"So did I," he whispered back. "She's the epitome of

discretion so don't worry." He glanced at his watch. "I've got to go pick up Maribelle—"

"I can do it."

"No, it's her first day and—"

"But I can. Seems like you're busy."

"Adelaide. We'll go together."

"Okay." It was progress that he'd want her to go along—at least from earlier that day. Except, if they went together and Sally was still there… She would be, wouldn't she? Sure, she would. She wouldn't miss another chance to see Ash. She might let something slip then since clearly, their past was on her brain.

Her warped, sick brain.

She hadn't been much better back then, had she?

He hoofed it to his office while she made good on her self-promise. It took her no time to empty the two bottles into the sink and down the drain. She stuffed them to the bottom of the trash.

Then, she jogged back upstairs to get real clothes on. Sally wanted to play mafia games? It wasn't a dead fish wrapped in newspaper, but her "gift" was most certainly a message. Fine, it was time for her to make her own hit.

While Ash casually leaned back in his large executive chair, visible from the entranceway, she snuck out of the house.

She'd left a note, saying she had errands to run and this would be a good time for him to have some father-daughter bonding. No need to tell him she was about to go to war—a long-overdue war.

Addy found Sally easily, almost too easily. She swung by the girl's academy front office, hoping she could somehow convince them to tell her where Sally might have gone next. Instead? She found the woman loitering there. Didn't this woman do anything other than hang around making trouble?

"Oh, look. It's Adelaide Bloom." She smiled blandly, oblivious to Addy's attempts to render her dead with her gaze. "But school isn't out for another—"

"Thirty minutes. I know. Got a minute? It's such a nice day out, I thought we could chat outside."

Her cheeks lifted in a cat-like smile. The woman thought she had the upper hand? *Ha.*

Sally followed Addy's march out to the school playground and the old swing set. She could scarcely believe the thing still stood there. Just like old times. She hated those times.

Addy spun on her. "How dare you?"

Sally had the nerve to look shocked. "What?"

"Leaving jalapeno juice on Ash's front stoop? Are you mad?"

"What are you going on about now, Addy?"

"You can't let me have a life, can you?"

The woman's mouth hung open and she scoffed. "A life? Oh, I get it. Ash Scott. You think he's going to ride off into the sunset. Get over yourself."

"No, you get over yourself. Today was a new low, even for you."

Sally sighed, closed her eyes. "Look, I know you and I have had a complicated past—"

"Complicated?" This woman was unbelievable. "Getting me fired?"

She shook her head and her forehead wrinkled. "What? Addy—"

"Don't Addy me."

"Well, it is your name."

"You and Bryson. Calling up my families, telling them…"

She stopped. She couldn't even voice how immature she'd been back then.

"Telling *your* families? Addy, honest to God, I don't know what you're talking about half the time." Sally sounded exasperated. "My brother cheated on you. You meted out an… *unusual* punishment. End of story. Now, if you don't mind, I am going back inside." A low *jeesh* emitted from under her breath as she turned away.

Not so fast. It was time they had this out. Sure, Addy had confronted her when "the incidents" actually happened but it never felt fully resolved. She grabbed Sally's arm. "You are seriously going to deny you and Bryson didn't—"

"Bryson and I what? We told the truth. Unlike you." Her lashes flicked upward to gaze behind her, then back down to Addy's face. She drew nearer. "Maybe it's time your boss learns why people need to be warned about you. You are a bit… sadistic." Her lip curled.

"Adelaide?" Ash's voice sounded behind her.

She closed her eyes, took in a breath, and pivoted to face him.

"Warn me about what?" Ash didn't hide his frustration.

Sally wasted no time filling in the details, of course. "Yes, I suppose you *didn't* tell your boss, Adelaide, how you landed my brother and his wife in the hospital, did you?" She dropped her arms and sidled up to him. "I'm sorry, Ash, I didn't want to be the one to say anything, but I should have. For Maribelle's sake."

"Oh, please," Addy said. "You don't give a rat's ass about her."

"Oh, I think Ash would be very interested in learning—"

"Shut. Your. Mouth. Sally." She turned to face Ash, whose face had turned to stone.

"I mean, what if the press learned?" Sally just had to put the last nail in Addy's coffin—as usual. Ash was terrified of more negative headlines. So, why not throw Adelaide Bloom under the bus again, show whatever negative thing someone got in their life was because of *her*.

His lips thinned to a straight line. "I'm getting Maribelle. Good day, ladies."

Yes, that's what they should do. "I'll follow you."

"No." He didn't look back again.

Addy jogged after him. "I'm sorry. I didn't mean—"

"*Adelaide*. Not now." She'd never seen him so angry. Pure wrath—that's what she saw in his eyes. How much had he overheard?

She backed up a few steps. "I'm—"

He raised a hand. "*I'm* not interested right now. I have to go get my daughter."

This was it, wasn't it? Why would he believe anything but it was Adelaide in the wrong?

The moment was so familiar. It unfolded the way it always did. Someone learned what happened nine years ago and they'd want nothing to do with her. She'd be fired. They'd never speak of it again. And she was so sick of that outcome every time. It was time to stop it.

"I quit," she shouted to his back. He'd kept walking, but she couldn't seem to make her feet work anymore. Her shoes felt filled with lead.

He stilled.

Kids were resilient, she reminded herself. Maribelle would forget about her. She'd bounce back. Just like Addy had and would again.

And honestly, quitting felt good, right. Normally, she'd stand there, waiting for whoever learned of her past to mete out punishment. Time to halt the throw-Addy-out game.

He slowly turned and presented his face, hard and unforgiving. A muscle twitched in his cheek. Still, the man was so beautiful. His dark hair lifted a little in the breeze. His blue eyes softened a tad at seeing her, but the disappointment coloring them nearly crushed her. He'd never look at her again with heat, with longing.

He was done. So was she.

She spun away and ran to her car. With every footfall, she left a piece of her heart on the ground—again.

28

Addy didn't get very far. She drove around Moorsville for a good thirty minutes, not quite knowing what to do next. Her phone kept ringing, Ash's number lighting up her screen.

She didn't have the courage to answer it. She knew what he'd do. Sally probably followed him inside. Filled in the gaps of what happened. So, he'd do what all the others did. Yell. Scream. Tell her all the things she'd heard before.

Irresponsible. Shocking. Immature.

She needed time to think, to figure out what to do next.

Go straight to Practically Perfect Nannies office? Yeah, Mrs. Dexter will be *so glad* to hear she threw this job in Ash's face. She'd warned her to stay professional. She'd done the exact opposite.

Go see Scarlett who would tell her to "just have fun with him?" Give up any idea on being with him with any permanence at all? Come to think of it, what was Addy thinking, getting involved with Ash on any level at all?

How about she drives to the airport, gets on a plane, and never comes back?

Instead, Addy picked up her phone and dialed Scarlett

anyway. She'd get an earful of finger-wagging at Addy's poor judgement, but maybe she'd understand why Addy would feel compelled to run at this point.

Maybe she'd lend her plane fare.

She pulled into the first parking lot she saw. "Marshall & Son Funeral Service. How appropriate," she muttered under her breath.

Scarlett answered on the first ring. "Okay, what the hell is going on? The Exalted One came looking for you." The clink of plates sounded in the background. She had to be at work at Peppermint Sweet.

"He did?"

"Something about you ran off. He seems really worried. He even bought Maribelle pie. The *blueberry*."

Okay, he was worried if he caved on that one. Nothing stained like blueberries. "I'll call him."

"By the way, did you get my present?"

"Present?" She chewed on the side of her thumb.

"The jalapeno juice. I mean, in case Ash decides—"

Her hand fell to her lap *hard*. "Scarlett! Tell me you didn't."

"I mean, not that I think he'd ever do something that warranted—"

"Shit, shit, shit, shit." She slapped her free hand on the steering wheel.

"What is going on with you?" Scarlett had the nerve to sound incredulous.

"I just accused Sally of leaving it."

A huge gasp sounded. "I only left it to remind you not to take any shit. I signed the note."

"An 'S.' You left an initial." How was she to know it stood for Scarlett? She sighed. Prickly Puss was more intelligent than she'd been today. "Scarlett, she brought up the... *incident*. In. Front. Of. Ash."

"Well, tell him what happened. He'd understand. He's probably seen worse."

"No. Way."

"Yes way. I can fix this. Hold on." The rustling of fabric sounded in Addy's ear. "Hey, Greta. Family emergency. Can I run out for an hour?"

A woman's voice was next, then Scarlett was back. "I'll meet you at Ash's place. He might know the big picture, but I'm sure not enough. You didn't tell him everything, did you?"

"Of course not," she hissed. Unlike a stuffed pink elephant, Addy had survival instincts.

"It's time. And if you don't, I will." Scarlett then killed the call.

Addy quickly pulled off and made an illegal U-turn. Scarlett was right. This was an emergency. Because if Addy didn't show up? Scarlett wouldn't be diplomatic about the story at all. Then he'd truly think she was a lunatic. Which she kind of was, now that she looked back on it.

When she pulled up to Ash's house, Scarlett, always a lead foot when it came to driving, was already in the driveway, leaning against her car.

Addy scrambled out of the car. "Please, let me handle this."

"Oh, you're going to handle it alright. You are Adelaide-fricking-Bloom." Her sister strode over to her, hooked her arm in hers, and pulled her toward the house. "You know what Dad always said. 'Courage is being scared to death…'"

"And saddling up anyway. John Wayne. I remember."

"And Ash has one mighty fine saddle, if I do say so myself. So, get back on his horse and…"

They both looked up and found Ash staring down at them from the top of the stairs. He did not look happy. "Let's talk inside."

He then led them to the dining room. Not his office, not the living room, but the freaking dining room, which spoke volumes. Her gig here was most definitely up because nothing said 'temporary' like the dining room.

"Where's Maribelle?" Her voice came out like a squeak.

"Taking a nap. It was a big day for her. A good one until…" He lifted his hand, palm up.

Guilt filled every inch of her body "I'm sorry. I didn't mean to run off like that. Sally brings out the worst in me, and I thought you'd never want to see me again. But then I found out that Scarlett—"

"Yep, the jalapeno juice was me. Meant to be kind of a half-joke." Scarlett half-laughed. "And I thought you'd get it, Addy," she hissed.

"It was not funny," she said through gritted teeth.

Scarlett rolled her eyes.

He scrubbed his hair. "What the devil is going on around here? What game are you two playing?"

Addy shook her head. "No game."

"Then start talking."

Scarlett waved her hand. "Okay, just keep an open mind."

"I'm an attorney. My mind is always open."

Scarlett winked at him. "Then you're going to love this."

Addy grabbed her arm and pulled her off to the side. "He might not."

"Bryson totally deserved it."

"Ash is not going to think that."

Scarlett tilted her head. "How good is his sense of humor?"

"You've met him." She raised her arm toward him and dropped it back to her side.

Ash stepped forward. "You do know I'm standing right here."

Addy sighed. "Okay." But how do you tell someone you

took revenge out on an ex? Generally, men frowned upon women going crazy on their ex-fiancés. "First, it was justified."

Ash crossed his arms and glared down at her, a mixture of puzzlement and impatience.

Scarlett leaned forward. "It was. Trust me."

Addy glared at her sister. "Let me handle this, okay?"

Scarlett raised both her hands in surrender.

She turned back to Ash. "You remember me telling you I was once engaged to Sally's brother, Bryson?"

"The first guy Addy went out with," Scarlett said. "after you snubbed her—"

"Scarlett."

"Well, it took her a long time to finally start dating. And why you picked a hometown boy, I'll never know. Anyway, when she did finally at the ripe old age of eighteen, well, he turned out to be an even bigger ass than you—"

"*Scarlett.*"

Scarlett made a wide sweeping motion with her hand. "Okay, okay. The floor is yours." She then eased herself onto the dining room table and swung her legs back and forth.

Addy chewed her lip and gazed up at his beautiful blue eyes, praying like hell he did have a deeper sense of humor than she'd encountered to date buried under his icy face. "I found him in bed with someone else."

Scarlett cleared her throat.

"Okay, two someones."

"Sarah Jean and Michael," Scarlett interjected.

"It doesn't matter. What *does* is it was one week before our wedding."

Ash dropped his arms and his nostrils flared. "That's unconscionable."

"It was." It was stunning how the old anger rose up like flames inside her. How she cracked open the door expecting to find Bryson sitting on the couch with his game controller in his hand, his smile wide when he saw her. Instead, she was greeted with an empty living room and grunts coming from the bedroom down the hallway. She shuddered at the memory. "Then he eloped with Sara Jean a few days later."

"They came back and had a party for everyone," Scarlett chuffed. "Everyone except us. I literally was told to take the night off on the busiest night they'd had in years."

"It's not polite to ask the ex and her family to your reception." Even if she'd wanted to drive a tank through the front window during it.

"Some reception. Cheapskates rented out Peppermint Sweet and made it an open house-like deal but everyone had to pay for their own stuff. Now, pay attention, because here is where it gets good. Since I work there, and we were tasked with delivering the wedding cake, we switched it out for *our* version of the cake they deserved. It was all your mother's idea—"

His forehead wrinkled. "What?"

Addy raised her hand to silence her sister. "She overheard me talking to my mom, who was not happy with what Bryson did. But, well, *your* mom then offered up a special cake pan for the cake."

"A cake mold." He said the words carefully as if he didn't understand. "My mother didn't bake."

"But she held parties here a lot for people. People used to leave stuff behind. There was this one bachelorette party for a daughter of a friend and they left…" God, how could she tell him this?

Scarlett beat her to the punch. "A penis mold. So, we swapped their original cake with a penis cake. Some of my best work. I even made it vegan. Sarah Jean already had enough meat on her plate."

That's when Ash lost it. He covered his eyes with one

hand and his entire body shook with laughter. He scrubbed his face and stared at Scarlett. "Tell me it was pink."

"Hot pink with black piping for the—"

Addy slapped her hand over her sister's mouth to stop her oversharing. And this next bit? Total overshare.

Ash suddenly sobered. "Wait. My mother? Are you sure?"

Scarlett pried Addy's hand from her face. "Hand to God. Mrs. Scott was cool. May she rest in peace."

"It seems you both knew her better than I did."

"She loved Addy… and my mom who worked here. I didn't as much. I prefer to be working with people."

A long second of silence passed between them. Addy chewed her lip and… waited. Finally, Ash pulled her into him. Her face mashed against his dress shirt. He pressed a kiss into her hair. "Oh, Addy."

"You're not mad?" Her words muffled in his shirt.

"Not the classiest response, but I agree. It *was* justified."

She pulled back and looked up at him. "You think?"

He smiled down at her. "I do. But I don't understand the hospital part. Tell me you didn't put something in the cake."

"Oh, no. But this is where it gets good," Scarlett said.

He held Addy out a foot, both hands on her biceps. "There's more?"

"Yeah." Addy's voice came out like a squeak. "But we don't need to go into it."

"What?" Scarlett pushed herself off the table. "The man understands. So, tell him all of it." She looked up at Ash. "Bryson got her fired after that. Told the family she wasn't fit to be around kids."

Addy could barely swallow the lump that formed in her throat. She'd loved that family. What hurt the most was how they didn't take her side. Sure, what she'd done was petty and probably uncalled for, but still…

"He had no right calling up your employer," Ash said.

She rubbed her throat as if that would loosen the muscles so she could talk. "It happened twice more. Sally, who I found out later also introduced Bryson to Sarah Jean and wanted *her* as a sister-in-law, not me, also called the families. She and her brother wanted to ruin me. So, as you can imagine, I had…" She turned away, couldn't look into his beautiful eyes. "*Ideas* on how to…" How did she frame this next part? Revenge? Getting even? An immature response to an untenable situation? It all seemed so petty now.

Scarlett sidled up to Addy. "Let me handle the rest. You look like you're going to throw up."

"Scarlett…"

"Then do it already."

Okay, here goes everything. She faced him again and let the words come out in a rush. "I snuck into his house. I still had the key. And I might have put something in his condoms. With a hypodermic needle."

Scarlett's smile widened. "Jalapeno juice. The lube, too. It was brilliant, if I do say so myself."

Ash pressed his lips together and his eyes widened. "Your idea, I take it?"

"The condoms were. The lube was allll Addy." She raised a hand seeking a high five. Addy ignored it. "Personally, I would have gone with ghost pepper juice, but on such short notice, we made do."

Addy studied the carpet. "I shouldn't have. I mean, he and Sarah Jean the next day had to go to the emergency room and…"

"A bunch of babies. Going to the emergency room? Pfft. Though, I'd have given good money to have overheard Fuck-face—excuse my language—explain how his dick was nearly burned off. With any luck, there's permanent scarring."

Addy sighed. "Not to worry. I looked up how bad it could be before… The damage would have been temporary at best."

Ash pinched the bridge of his nose. "Oh my God." He didn't look happy, but then again, men usually cringed at the thought of their manly bits having any vulnerability at all. Even if it wasn't *their* manly bits being *fired up*.

Shit, she was going to be fired for real now. Sure, she'd quit, but she kinda held out hope he'd beg her to come back.

He sighed heavily, dropped his arm, and his gaze finally returned to her face. "That's brilliant."

Scarlett lifted her eyebrows at Addy. "Told ya' he'd understand." She placed her hand on Ash's bicep. "I'm proud of you, Ashton Scott. You do your mother proud."

He instantly sobered and pointed his finger at her. "But they could have sued for damages."

"Again," Scarlett said lightly. "Would have paid money to hear him explain those damages in a courtroom. Whip it out as evidence…"

"Scarlett," both she and Ash said in unison.

"Now, you two… make-up sex time." She kissed Addy on the cheek. "Remember the details." She turned and strode to the door. "Now, if you ever need a penis cake, you know where to find me. I still have the mold." She twirled her hand in the air.

Addy stood stock-still, waiting for Ash to speak. He didn't, not even when the sound of the front door closed.

Addy swallowed and stared up at him. "So…"

Still no response. His smile had dropped. *Uh, oh.* They were alone now, so maybe he was merely being polite around Scarlett. But since when did anyone feel the need to be polite around her?

He ran his hand down her arm and captured her hand. "Okay. Here's the deal…"

She straightened. How could she still find his stern voice so hot when she was about to be dumped?

"Let me tell you something. When someone I care about

is threatened, I will go to the ends of the earth to protect them. I mean, for that reason, I ended up here."

"Moorsville's not the end of the earth. I mean, it's not Manhattan—"

"It's better."

He did not say that. "It is?"

"I can't believe it, but yes, in some ways. Now." He stepped backward and let go of her hand. "I hate to do this, but…" He sucked in a long breath. "Adelaide Bloom, you're fired."

A roaring silence filled her body like a windstorm was running through her, taking everything, hollowing her out. It was a strange feeling. She thought when he inevitably dropped her, it'd crush her. It didn't. It was worse.

This really was the end, wasn't it? She'd told him the worst of herself, and he'd passed his judgement on her. He didn't want her around anymore.

He'd been like everyone else. For so many years he'd been the man she held everyone else accountable to. What a fool. He was like all the others. Who was it that said when someone shows you who they are, believe them? The writer's name was on the tip of her tongue when his hand grasped her chin. Not roughly but with conviction.

"I realize now that you can't be the nanny and be… more," he said.

Her lashes couldn't stop fluttering. More?

He then yanked her flush to him and sealed his lips over hers.

When he finally released his kiss, her nerves were dancing. "I don't understand…"

He swiped the hair off her forehead. "I can't recall a time when I've enjoyed life as much as I have since running into you at the agency."

Her mind raced back in time. "But I gave Maribelle pie."

"I forgive you. Now, about us…" He released her, stepped back, and stared at her hard. "Are you in or are you out?"

"In?" She squeaked.

"Good. But—"

"No, I won't marry you. You can beg all you want…" Jesus, her mouth. Where did it come up with this stuff?

It was his turn to blink and appear stunned. He shifted on his feet. He was… embarrassed? Oh, my God. Could Scarlett be right? He did want her and didn't quite know what to do with it.

"How about we start with girlfriend?" he finally asked. "Just one thing." He recaptured her hand. "Leave the jalapeno juice at home?"

"I would never do something like that again."

"I shall endeavor never to give you reason to."

She laughed at his formal words. "I'm sure you won't. And if you're worried about Maribelle—"

"I'm not." His thumb massaged the inside of her hand. "For the first time in a year, I'm not worried for her. I have you to thank for that."

"But what about New York?"

"I can still go back in the middle of the week for a few days but make this place home base. I want to be around for Maribelle. I want her to have a different childhood than I did." He glanced around. "Besides, I rather like it here. It's kind of grown on me."

"Told ya'."

"Don't let it go to your head, girlfriend."

Her eyes stung. This was happening. She was Ash Scott's *girlfriend*. "What made you change your mind?"

He looked puzzled. "Change my mind? I didn't."

"But, on the playground…" A silly laugh bubbled up at saying the word "playground."

"I was angry. Not exactly at you, but I abhor gossip. I

don't care what you did back then, Adelaide, unless it was illegal. But what your ex did to you was reprehensible. I've been hired to get justice for less."

She shrugged. "I didn't know any lawyers back then." As if that would have made any difference.

"Well, you do now. I'll give you a great reference for your next job, and if anyone…" His voice held so much conviction she had to swallow. "And I mean anyone tries to hurt you again, they deal with me."

She almost asked, 'Even Sally?' but wisely didn't. "I owe Sally an apology. I think. I'll do it tomorrow."

"If you wish to."

"You don't care either way?"

He shook his head slowly. "No. I care about you."

"But the academy and Maribelle—"

"They're lucky to have her."

They were, actually.

"Like we're lucky to have you. If you're willing to stay in Maribelle's life, I welcome it. If…"

"If what?" She needed to know his conditions because if he had any, she might be setting herself up again. "Please, don't ask me to follow the *Child Genius* book. Or worse, you want me to do the supermodel thing? I can't. No makeup. No high heels that, quite frankly, will ruin your feet. And I look terrible in jersey fabric. How anyone looks good in that I'll never know. I mean, it shows everything, like ev-er-y—"

Her words were silenced in only the way Ash could: his mouth closed over hers. He kissed her so hard and for so long she completely forgot if he'd asked her a question at all.

When he pulled back, his beautiful eyes shone down on her, smiling. "Yes. I'm going to have to do that *a lot*."

"Uh-huh."

"That is… if you'll have me."

Have him? Was he out of his blooming mind? She jumped

up and wrapped her legs around him. "Try to go *anywhere* without me. Remember. I am very creative."

He then spun her and placed her on the dining room table. "So am I."

Then, Ash Scott, The Exalted One with a tongue that truly should be patented, did things to her on the dining room table that would have appalled Mrs. Scott. Like, seriously shocked.

Maybe. She'd ask her painting about it someday where it hung in Addy's very, very lucky hallway.

EPILOGUE

Addy stared at the sunlight peeking through the tree leaves overhead. "They're all going to turn copper and yellow soon."

Maribelle held up Miss Charlotte to show her. "See? Even the trees love our favorite color." She dropped her doll dramatically to her side. "Daddy, are you done *yet*?"

Ash's face peered over the edge of the tree castle, now completely finished. "Okay, ladies, come on up." The wooden ladder unfolded down to the ground.

Addy lifted her up so her feet landed on the first rung. "You first, Queen Maribelle."

She pushed her doll into Addy's face. "Can you hold her? She gets scared alone. We're coming, Daddy."

Addy spit Miss Charlotte's hair out of her face and tucked the doll under her arm. She followed Maribelle slowly up the ladder, praying like hell the wood didn't give way under both of them. Turned out Ash built quite the sturdy ladder.

He'd built quite the castle, too. A wide platform took up most of the space, but he'd also included a small room along the back with a high roof that, if you squinched your eyes, could be considered a turret. Good thing Maribelle wasn't too picky except for the color. The room part of the structure was an eye-searing bright yellow.

Maribelle scrambled onto the platform, turned and held out her arms for her doll. Addy gave the poor thing to her. Miss Charlotte's hair was a knotted mess, thanks to her weekly "salon appointments." Her little white apron also was stained with… something.

Ash hadn't found a new nanny, after all—and somehow she just never left despite several offers.

"Hey, Belle, why don't you scoot over?" Ash pulled her closer to him and Maribelle laid her head on his chest.

It tugged on Addy's heart as it always did, seeing the two of them together, growing closer every day. Maribelle loved school, and she and Ash, when he was in town, had "tea" every afternoon where he got an earful over which little girl was in *looove* with which little boy.

Man, they started early.

Maribelle waved her hand. "Okay, start, Daddy."

"What are we starting?" Addy grunted a little as she settled on the wide platform. "A christening of the castle?" She pointed at the little picnic Ash had set out. A French country tablecloth with a cheery yellow, blue, and lime green design was splayed out over half the small space. A bottle of champagne sat in a sweating ice bucket in the middle along with a charcuterie board and a cherry pie.

He and Maribelle exchanged a glance. "You could say that," Ash said.

"We must be if you brought pie," she laughed.

"The pie was important. I mean, for…"

Maribelle put a finger to her lips. "Daddy," she whispered. "On your knees."

"In due time, Belle."

She sighed and moved to sitting cross-legged.

"What's going on, you two?" Addy took a cube of cheese

and placed it into her mouth. "Mmm, my favorite. Extra sharp cheddar. Oh, and dark chocolate almonds." She grabbed one of those, too.

Maribelle fidgeted. "Time for tea."

Ash chuckled. "With pie?"

Addy picked up the triangle-shaped server. "Always time for pie." She went to work cutting up small-ish pieces while Maribelle served the tea. She'd brought her plastic set out to join the picnic.

She handed Ash a piece of pie, who amazingly took it. He stared at her, his face unreadable. "Don't tell me you don't want it. I mean, that," she pointed at the piece on his plate, "is legendary."

"No, you are." He looked so serious it made her sit up tall.

"You been listening to my sister again?" Turned out she and Ash had reached some kind of understanding. Scarlett visited every weekend. They'd then trade the dirtiest jokes they'd learned over the week. Ash wasn't as formal as Addy had made him out to be. Then again, Scarlett brought out the smutty in everyone's minds if you spent enough time with her.

He set down his pie untouched. "I don't need anyone to tell me that. You are amazing, Adelaide."

Okay, something was really up. "What happened?"

One side of his mouth inched up. "Nothing. Yet."

"Am in trouble?"

"Daddy," Maribelle whispered. She pointed to the floor.

He chuckled, then rose up on his knees. He inched forward and lifted a little teacup. "Maribelle and I would like you to have some of this magic tea."

She arched an eyebrow on purpose. Ash hadn't bought into her magic ways yet—well, except for in the bedroom. He made her see stars often enough the man had to be a wizard in disguise. She took the cup and made a pretend sipping motion. Something tinkled inside.

She glanced down. No. Way. She looked back up at Ash.

"Adelaide Bloom, would you please resign as being a nanny for anyone ever again? Instead…"

Maribelle jumped up and threw herself at Addy and wrapped her arms around her, tipping her off-balance. "Be my mommy instead."

Addy caught Maribelle with one hand, holding out the teacup.

Ash grabbed it, then something cold and metal slipped onto her finger. She glanced down.

Yep. She hadn't imagined the huge diamond at all.

"Marry me?" he asked.

"Oh, my God." Her hand flew to her lips and the diamond slipped to the side. It would. It was the size of a gumball.

"Well, that wasn't exactly the response I'd—"

"Yes, I'll marry you." She hoped her words were audible because her throat was clogging. She cleared the lump as best she could. "I mean, this doesn't mean I'm going to ever let you start winning a water balloon fight or change my mind on getting Maribelle a pony—"

His lips pressed against hers. "I love you," he said into her mouth, pressing Maribelle between them. A muffled, little-girl giggle sounded against her chest.

"Love you, too," she squeaked.

Maribelle pushed against her and sighed dramatically. "Can we have pie now?"

He sat back. "Yes. Pie. In fact, something tells me we'll be having more from now on. The brain needs glucose, after all." He winked at her.

"Someone's been reading the *Genius Child* book," she whispered.

"Nah. I got rid of those." He forked a huge piece of pie.

Addy looked down at the ring on her finger, the diamond sparkling in the light. The solitaire was so large it would never sit right on her finger. She'd have to fiddle with it to keep it in place. Maybe it'd be a constant reminder that the past doesn't equal the future.

Which was a very good thing because she wasn't ever dusting his dining room again, even if he did put a ring on it.

She massaged the side of her neck, as if that might dislodge the emotion trying to escape from her throat.

"Do you like it? It was my mother's." Ash's voice was quiet. "I think she'd want you to have it, too."

He'd caught her staring at her hand. She looked up into his beautiful blue eyes, and her breath hitched. "Your mom's. It's perfect." Now it did fit. Everything did.

Thank you for reading The Sassy Nanny Dilemma.
An honest review of the story is always welcome.

Never miss a new release from Elizabeth! Visit
ElizabethSaFleur.com to sign up for her newsletter.

ABOUT THE AUTHOR

Elizabeth SaFleur writes award-winning, luscious romance from 28 wildlife-filled acres, hikes in her spare time and is ruled by a 17lb Westie.

Find out more about Elizabeth on her web site at <u>www. ElizabethSaFleur</u> or join her private Facebook group, Elizabeth's Playroom.

Follow her on TikTok (@ElizabethSaFleurAuthor) and Instagram (@ElizabethLoveStory), too!

ALSO BY ELIZABETH SAFLEUR

Sexy rom-coms:

The Sassy Nanny Dilemma

It Was All The Pie's Fault

It Was All the Cat's Fault

It Was All the Daisy's Fault

For You, Anything

Kiss a Ginger Day

Short story collections:

Finally, Yours

Finally, His

Finally, Mine

Steamy Contemporary romance:

Tough Luck

Tough Break

Tough Love

Erotic romance with BDSM:

Elite

Holiday Ties (short story)

Untouchable

Perfect

Riptide (novella)

Lucky

Fearless

Invincible

Femme Domme:

The White House Gets A Spanking

Spanking the Senator